W9-BAI-487

THE HEIR'S
CHOSEN BRIDE

THE HEIR'S CHOSEN BRIDE

BY

MARION LENNOX

MILLS & BOON®

All the characters in this book have no existence outside
the imagination of the author, and have no relation
whatsoever to anyone bearing the same name or names.
They are not even distantly inspired by any individual
known or unknown to the author, and all the incidents
are pure invention.

All Rights Reserved including the right of reproduction
in whole or in part in any form. This edition is published
by arrangement with Harlequin Enterprises II B.V. The
text of this publication or any part thereof may not be
reproduced or transmitted in any form or by any means,
electronic or mechanical, including photocopying,
recording, storage in an information retrieval system,
or otherwise, without the written permission of
the publisher.

MILLS & BOON and
MILLS & BOON with the Rose Device
are registered trademarks of the publisher.

First published in Great Britain 2006
Large Print edition 2006
Harlequin Mills & Boon Limited,
Eton House, 18-24 Paradise Road,
Richmond, Surrey TW9 1SR

© Marion Lennox 2006

ISBN-13: 978 0 263 19018 2
ISBN-10:   0 263 19018 8

Set in Times Roman 15½ on 17¾ pt.
16-1106-58636

Printed and bound in Great Britain
by Antony Rowe Ltd, Chippenham, Wiltshire

CHAPTER ONE

Information required on whereabouts of Dougal Douglas (or direct descendant), brother to Lord Angus Douglas, Earl of Loganaich. Contact solicitors Baird and O'Shannasy, Dolphin Bay, Australia, for information to your advantage.

'MR DOUGLAS, you're an earl.'

Hamish groaned. He was hours behind schedule. The Harrington Trust Committee was arriving in thirty minutes and his perky secretary-in-training was driving him nuts.

'Just sort the mail.'

'But this letter says you're an earl. You gotta read it.'

'Like I read e-mails from Nigeria offering to share millions. All I need to do is send my bank account details. Jodie, you know better.'

'Of course I do,' she told him indignantly. Honestly, he was being a twit.

But she forgave him. Who wouldn't? Hamish Douglas was the cutest boss she'd ever worked for. Jodie had been delighted when Marjorie had retired and she'd been given the chance to take her place. At thirty-three, Hamish was tall, dark and drop-dead gorgeous. He had ruffled black curls, which fought back when he tried to control them. He had deep brown twinkly eyes and the most fantastic smile…

When he smiled. Which wasn't often. Hamish might be one of the most brilliant young futures brokers in Manhattan, but he didn't seem to enjoy life.

Maybe he'd smile when he realised he really was an earl.

'This one's different,' she told him. 'Honest, Mr Douglas, you need to look. If you're who these people think you are then you've inherited a significant estate. A significant estate in lawyer speak…I bet that means a fortune.'

'I've inherited nothing. It's a scam.'

'What's a scam? Is Jodie bothering you with nuisance mail?'

Uh-oh. Jodie had been rising, but as soon as the door opened she sat straight back down. Marcia Vinel was Hamish's fiancée. Trouble. Jodie had overheard Marcia on at least two occasions advising Hamish to get rid of her.

'She's a temp from the typing pool. Surely you can do better.'

'But I like her,' Hamish had replied, much to Jodie's delight. 'She's smart, intuitive and organised—and she makes me laugh.'

'Your secretary's not here to make you laugh,' Marcia had retorted.

No, Jodie thought, shoving the offending letter into the tray marked PENDING. Life's too serious to laugh. Life's about making money.

'What's the letter?' Marcia said, with a sideways glance at Jodie to say she didn't appreciate Jodie knowing anything about Hamish that she herself didn't. 'Is it a scam?'

Jodie knew when to turn into a good secretary. She tugged on her headset, paid attention to her keyboard and didn't answer. 'What's the letter?' Marcia said again, this time directly to Hamish.

'It's some sort of con,' Hamish said wearily. 'And Jodie's not bothering me any more than anyone else is. Hell, Marcia, I have work to do.'

'I came to tell you the Harrington delegation's been delayed,' Marcia told him. 'Their flight's two hours late from London. Relax.'

He did, but not much. That meant rescheduling and…

'I'll rearrange your appointments.' Jodie emerged

from her headset and he cast her a look of gratitude. 'Only I do think you should read the letter.' She mightn't like Marcia, she decided, but at least Marcia would make Hamish look at it.

He went back to frowning. 'Jodie, get real. Letters saying I'm an earl and I've inherited a fortune are the stuff of a kid's fantasy.'

'But it doesn't say send bank account details. It says contact a solicitor. That sounds fusty rather than scammy. Real.'

'Let me see,' Marcia decreed, and put out an imperious hand. Marcia was a corporate lawyer working for the same company as Hamish. She was the brains, he was the money, some people said— but Hamish had earned his money with his wits, and there was a fair bit of cross-over.

The two were a team. Jodie handed it over.

There was silence while Marcia read. The letter was on the official notepaper of an Australian legal firm. It looked real, Jodie thought defiantly. She wasn't wasting her boss's time.

And Marcia didn't think so either. She finished reading and set the letter down with an odd look on her face.

'Hamish, do you have an uncle called Angus Douglas? In Australia?'

'No.' He frowned. 'Or...I don't think so.'

'Surely you know your uncles,' Jodie said, and got a frown from Marcia for her pains. She subsided but she didn't replace her headset.

'My father migrated from Scotland when he was little more than a kid,' Hamish told Marcia. 'There was some sort of family row—I don't know what. He never told my mother anything about his family and he died when I was three.'

'You never enquired?' Marcia demanded, astounded, as if such disinterest was inexcusable.

'About what?'

'About his background. Whether he was wealthy?'

'He certainly wasn't wealthy. He migrated just after the war when every man and his dog was on the move from Europe. He married my mother and they had nothing.' He hesitated. 'All I know…'

'All you know is what?' said Marcia, still staring at the letter.

'While I was at college my roommate was doing a history major. I went through some shipping lists he was using, just to see if I could find him. I did. Apparently my father left Glasgow in 1947 on the *Maybelline*. There was no other Douglas on the passenger list so I assumed he was alone.'

'Maybe he had a brother who migrated as well,' Marcia said thoughtfully. 'Maybe his brother went to Australia instead. Honey, this letter says someone called Angus Douglas, Earl of Loganaich, died six weeks ago in Australia and they're looking for relations of Dougal Douglas. Your father was Dougal, wasn't he?'

Hamish's face stilled.

'What?' Marcia said, and Jodie watched her face change. She knew that look. She'd seen it when Marcia was closing on a corporate deal. The look said she could smell money.

'There probably aren't that many Dougal Douglases,' Hamish said slowly. 'But…my father's address on the shipping manifest was Loganaich. I'd never heard of the place. I looked it up, and it's tiny. I thought some day I might go find it, but…'

'But you got busy,' Marcia said, approving. He certainly had. Hamish had been one of the youngest graduates ever to gain a first-class commerce-law degree from Harvard. After that had come his appointment with one of the most prestigious broking firms in New York, and he'd whizzed up the corporate ladder with the speed of light. At thirty-three, Hamish was a full partner and a millionaire a couple times over. There'd been no time in his fast-moving history for a leisurely stroll around Scotland. 'Hamish, this means you really might have inherited.'

'This is cool.' Jodie beamed, forgetting her dislike

of Marcia as imagination took flight. 'The letter says they're not sure whether they have the right person, but it does fit. It says your father was one of three brothers who left Scotland in 1947. The oldest two went to Australia and your dad came here.'

'He can read it for himself,' Marcia snapped and handed it over to Hamish.

'It'll be a scam.'

'Read it,' Marcia snapped.

And Jodie thought, Whoa, don't do that, lady. If Hamish was my guy I wouldn't talk like that.

But Hamish didn't notice. 'It's probably nothing,' he said at last, but dismissal had made way for uncertainty. 'But with the Loganaich connection... Maybe we should check.'

'I'll make enquiries about this law firm,' Marcia said. 'I'll get onto it straight away.'

'There's no need...'

'There certainly is,' Jodie breathed. 'Oh, Mr Douglas, the letter says you're an earl and you've inherited a castle and everything. How ace would that be? A Scottish earl. You might get to wear a kilt.'

'No one's seeing my knees,' Hamish said. He grinned—and then the phone rang and a fax came through that he'd been waiting for and he went back to work.

Castles and titles had to wait.

* * *

'They think they've found him.'

Susie Douglas, née McMahon, was sitting on a rug before the fire in the great hall of Loganaich-Castle-the-Second, playing with her baby. Rose Douglas was fourteen months old. She'd been tumbling with her aunt's dog, Boris, but now baby and dog had settled into a sleepy, snuggly pile, and the women were free to talk.

'The lawyers have been scouring America,' Susie told her twin. 'Now they think they've found the new earl. As soon as he comes, I…I think I'll go home.'

'But you can't.' Kirsty stared at her twin with horror. 'This is your home.'

'It's been great,' Susie said, staring round the fantastically decorated walls with affection. The two suits of armour guarding the hallway were wonderful all by themselves. She talked to them all the time. *Good morning, Eric. Good morning, Ernst.* 'But I can't live here for ever. It doesn't belong to me. I agreed to stay until Angus died, and now he has.' She took a deep breath. 'I've been marking time for too long, Kirsty, love. Eric and Ernst belong to someone else. It's time I moved on.'

'You mustn't.' Yet there was a part of Kirsty that knew Susie was right. This moment had been inevitable.

Susie had come so far... After the death of her husband, Rory, Susie had fallen apart, suffering from crippling depression as well as the injuries she'd received in the crash that had killed her husband. In desperation Kirsty had brought her to Australia to meet Rory's uncle. Lord Angus Douglas, Earl of Loganaich. It had been a grand title for a wonderful old man. In the earl they'd found a true friend, and in his outlandish castle Susie had recovered. She'd given birth to her daughter and she'd started to look forward again.

To home?

Susie's home was in America. Her landscaping business was in America. Now Angus was dead there was nothing keeping her here.

But while Susie had been recovering. Kirsty, her twin, had been falling in love with the local doctor. Kirsty and Jake now had a rambling house on the edge of town, kids, hens, dog—the whole domestic catastrophe. Kirsty's home was solidly here.

'I don't want you to go,' Kirsty whispered. 'Angus should have left this place to you.'

'He couldn't.'

'I don't see why not.'

'This castle was built with entailed money,' Susie explained. 'After the original Scottish castle burned down, the family trust made money available for re-

building. Angus managed to arrange it so he rebuilt
the castle here in Australia, but he still couldn't
leave it away from the true line of the peerage. If
I'd had a son it'd be different, but now it goes to a
nephew no one knows. It belongs to a Hamish
Douglas. An American.'

She said 'an American' in a tone of such disgust
that Kirsty burst out laughing. 'You sound as if
Americans are some sort of experimental bug,' she
said. 'Just remember you are one, Susie Douglas.'

'I hardly feel American any more,' Susie said,
sighing. Rose rolled sleepily off Boris, and Susie
scooped her baby daughter up to hug her. 'I have my
own little Australian.'

'Half American, half Scottish, born in Australia.
But she belongs here.'

'You see, I'm not sure any more,' Susie said,
sighing again. 'Angus has left me enough to buy a
little house and live happily ever after here. But I
need to work and there's not a lot of landscape gardening to be had in Dolphin Bay.'

'There's me,' Kirsty said defensively, and Susie
smiled.

'You know that counts for a lot. But not everything. I need a job, Kirsty. Rory's been dead for
almost two years. My injuries from the crash are
almost completely resolved. I loved caring for

Angus, but without him the castle seems empty. The only thing keeping me occupied is the upkeep on the castle and the garden, and once the new earl arrives…'

'When is he arriving?'

'I don't know,' Susie told her. 'But the lawyers say they've found him and told him he's inherited. If you were told you'd inherited a title and a fortune, wouldn't you hotfoot it over here?'

Kirsty gave a bleak little smile at that. So much sorrow had gone into this fortune, this title…

'I guess I would,' she admitted.

'Once he arrives there's nothing for me to do,' Susie told her, twirling the curls of her almost sleeping daughter.

'Maybe he won't come,' Kirsty said, trying not to sound desperate. She wanted her sister to stay so much. 'Or maybe he'll want you to stay as caretaker.'

'And leave it earning nothing? What would you do if you inherited this place?' Susie asked.

'Sell it as a hotel,' Kirsty said bluntly, and though she added a grimace it was no less than the truth. Angus had built this place when his castle back in Scotland had burned to the ground. The old man's whim had led him to rebuild here, in this magic place where the climate was so much kinder than Scotland's. But now…the castle seemed straight out of a fairy tale. It was far too big for a family. Angus had known it could be sold as a hotel, and his intention was surely about to be realised.

'It feels like a home,' Kirsty added stubbornly, and Susie laughed.

'Right. Fourteen bedrooms, six bathrooms, a banquet hall, a ballroom and me and Rose. Even if you and Jake and the kids and Boris came to live with us, we'd have three bedrooms apiece. It's crazy to think of staying.'

'But you can't go back,' Kirsty said again, and her twin's face grew solemn.

'I think I must.'

'At least stay and meet the new earl. Maybe he'll have some ideas rather than selling. Maybe he could employ you to make the garden better.'

'We both know that's a pipe dream.'

'But you will stay until he gets here. That's what Angus would have wanted.'

'I miss Angus so much,' Susie said softly, and her twin moved across to give her a swift hug.

'Oh, love. Of course you do.'

'The new laird might not even grow pumpkins,' Susie said sadly, and Kirsty had to smile.

'Unforgivable sin!'

'We've got the biggest this year,' Susie said, brightening. 'Did I tell you, the night before Angus died I snuck into Ben Boyce's yard and measured his. It's a tiddler in comparison. Angus died knowing he would definitely win this year's trophy.'

'There you go,' Kirsty said stoutly. 'The new earl just has to collect his pumpkin and take over where Angus left off.'

'The lawyers say he's some sort of financier. An American financier valuing a prize pumpkin...you have to be kidding.'

'I'm not kidding,' Kirsty said. 'You'll see. He'll come and he'll fall for the place and want a caretaker and landscape gardener extraordinaire, and pumpkin pie for dinner for the rest of his life.'

'He won't.'

'At least wait and see,' Kirsty begged. 'Please, Susie. You must give him a chance.'

'Holiday?' Hamish glared at his secretary in stupefaction. 'You are joking.'

'I'm not joking. Your holiday starts next week—sir. Oh, by the way, I'm quitting.'

'You're not making sense.' Hamish was late for a meeting. He'd been gathering his notes when his unconventional secretary had burst in to tell him her news.

'You're having three weeks' holiday starting next week,' Jodie repeated patiently. 'And I'm quitting.'

He gazed at her as he'd gaze at someone with two heads.

'You can't quit,' he said weakly, and she grinned.

'Yes, I can. I'm only a temp. I came here two years ago on a two-week agency placing, and no one's given me a contract.'

'But people don't just leave—'

'Well, why would they when the money's brilliant?' Jodie acknowledged. 'But have you noticed that people *do* leave this firm? They start taking time off because they can't cope. They're constantly tired. They forget things. They stop being efficient and then they're bumped. So all I'm doing is leaving before I'm bumped. Why do you think Marjorie retired so young? Listening to you and the girlfriend made me think…'

'Me and Marcia?'

'You and Marcia. She's as pleased as could be about your new title—she can't wait to get married so she'll be Lady Marcia Douglas—but as for agreeing you don't have time to go see a castle…'

'It's a fake castle,' he said faintly.

'A castle is a castle and it sounds cool,' Jodie declared. 'Just because it's not six hundred years old doesn't mean it's not a real one. And Marcia's idea of putting it on the market without seeing it is ridiculous. Anyway, I was talking to Nick, and he said—'

'Nick?'

'My partner,' she said with exaggerated patience. 'The man I share my life with. He's a woodworker. He was a social worker with disadvantaged kids, but the work just wore him out. He loved it but it exhausted him. He's almost as cute as you, and I talk about him all the time. Not that you listen.'

Hamish blinked. He hesitated and glanced at his watch. Then he carefully laid his papers on the desk in front of him. Jodie was a great, if unconventional, secretary, and it'd be more efficient to spend a few minutes now persuading her to stay rather than training someone new—

'Don't do this to me,' Jodie begged. 'You're scheduling me into your morning and I don't intend to be scheduled. I'm working on changing your life here. Not the next half-hour.'

'Pardon?'

'You see nothing but work,' she told him. 'The typing-pool gossip is that you've been blighted in love. That explains Marcia but it's none of my business. All I know is that you're blinkered. You've been given the most fantastic opportunity and you're throwing it away.'

Hamish sat down. 'This is—'

'Impertinent,' she told him, and beamed. 'I know. But someone needs to tell you. Nick's been given a contract to rebuild the choir stalls at a gorgeous old church up in New England. We're both going to move. That's why I need to quit. So then I thought if I was quitting I should try to save you first. Nick agrees. Spending your whole life making money is awful. Owning a castle and not visiting it before you sell it is madness. So I've cancelled every one of your appointments for the next three weeks, starting the minute you've finished with the Harrington committee. I haven't just crossed them out of your diary but I've contacted everyone and rescheduled. Job's done. As of next week I'm out of here, and if you have the brains I credit you with, so will you be.'

'I can't.'

'Yes, you can,' she told him. 'Your Lordship.'

'Jodie…'

'Yes?' She was beaming, as if she'd just played Santa Claus. 'I've booked flights for you. From JFK to Sydney, and there's a hire car waiting so you can drive straight down to Dolphin Bay. If you want to take Marcia they're holding two seats, but I told them you'd probably cancel one.'

'Marcia won't come.'

'No, but you will,' she told him. 'You've been in this job for nearly ten years, and no one can remember you taking a holiday. Oh, sure, you've

been away but it's always been on some financial
wheeler dealer arrangement. Dealing with Swiss
bankers with a little skiing on the side. A week on
a corporate yacht with financiers and oilmen. Not a
sniff of time spent lying on the beach doing nothing.
Isn't it about time you had a look at life before you
marry Marcia and…?' She paused and bit back what
she'd been about to say. 'And settle down?'

'I can't,' he said again, but suddenly he wasn't so
sure.

'I've cleared it with all the partners. Everyone
knows you're going and they know why. You've inherited a castle. Everyone's asking for postcards. So
you're going to look pretty dumb sitting round this
office for the next three weeks doing nothing. Or
telling everyone that I've lied about you needing a
holiday and you're not taking one, yah, boo, sucks.'

'Pardon?' he said again, and her grin widened.

'That's not stockbroker talk,' she told him. 'It's street
talk. Real talk. Which I've figured you need. If you're
going to go from share-broking to aristocracy maybe
you need a small wedge of real life in between.'

'Look, you dumb worm, if you don't get out of
there you'll be concrete.'

Susie's hair was escaping from her elastic band
and drifting into her eyes. She flipped it back with

the back of her hand, and a trickle of muddy water slid down her face. Excellent.

This was her very favourite occupation. Digging in mud. Susie was making a path from the kitchen door to the conservatory. The gravel path had sunk and she needed to pour concrete before she laid pavers, but first she had to dig. She'd soaked the soil to make it soft, and it was now oozing satisfactorily between her fingers as she rescued worms. Rose was sleeping soundly just through the window. The sun was shining on her face and she was feeling great.

She needed to get these worms out of the mud or they'd be cactus.

'I'm just taking you to the compost,' she told them, in her best worm-reassuring tone. 'The compost is worm heaven. Ooh, you're a nice fat one…'

A hand landed on her shoulder.

She was wearing headphones and had heard nothing. She yelped, hauled her headphones off, staggered to her feet and backed away. Fast.

A stranger was watching her with an expression of bemusement.

He might be bemused but so was she. The stranger looked like he'd just strolled off the deck of a cruising yacht. An expensive yacht. He was elegantly casual, wearing cream chinos and a white polo top with a discreet logo on the breast.

He was too far away now to tell what the logo was, but she bet it was some expensive country club. A fawn loafer jacket slung elegantly over one shoulder.

He was wearing cream suede shoes.

Cream shoes. Here.

She looked past the clothes with an effort—and there was surely something to see beside the clothes. The stranger was tall, lean and athletic. Deep black hair. Good skin, good smile…

Great smile.

She'd left the outer gate open. There was a small black sedan parked in the forecourt, with a hire-car company insignia on the side. She'd been so intent on her worms that he'd crept up on her unawares.

He could have been an axe murderer, she thought, a little bit breathless. She should have locked the gate.

But…maybe she was expecting him? This had to be who she thought he was. The new earl.

Maybe she should have organised some sort of guard of honour. A twelve-gun salute.

'You're the gardener?' he asked, and she tried to wipe mud away with more mud as she smiled back. She was all the welcome committee there was, so she ought to try her best.

A spade salute?

'I am the gardener,' she agreed. 'Plus the rest.

General dogsbody and bottle-washer for Loganaich Castle. What can I do for you?'

But his gaze had been caught. Solidly distracted. He was staring at a huge golden ball to the side of the garden. A vast ball of bright orange, about two yards wide.

'What is that?' he said faintly.

She beamed. 'A pumpkin. Her name's Priscilla. Isn't she the best?'

'I don't believe it.'

'You'd better. She's a Dills Atlantic Giant. We decided on replacing Queensland Blues this year— we spent ages on the Internet finding the really huge suckers—and went for Dills instead. Of course, they're not quite as good to eat. Actually, they're cattle feed, but who's worrying?'

'Not me,' he said faintly.

'The only problem is we need a team of body-builders to move her. Our main competitor has moved to Dills as well, but he doesn't have the expertise. We'll walk away with the award for Dolphin Bay's biggest pumpkin this year, no worries.'

'No worries,' he repeated, dazed.

'That's Australian for "no problem",' she explained kindly. 'Or you could say, "She'll be right, mate."'

This conversation was going nowhere. He tried to

get a grip. 'Is anyone home? In there?' He waved vaguely in the direction of the castle.

'I'm home. Me and Rose.'

'Rose?'

'My daughter. Are you—'

'I'm Hamish Douglas. I'm looking for a Susie Douglas.'

'Oh.'

He really was the new earl.

There was a moment's charged silence. She wasn't what he'd expected, she thought, but, then, he wasn't what she'd expected either.

She'd thought he'd look like Rory.

He didn't look like any of the Douglases she'd met, she decided. He was leaner, finer boned, finer...tuned? He was a Porsche compared to Rory's Land Rover, she decided, limping across to greet him properly. She still had residual stiffness from the accident in which Rory had been killed, and it was worse when she'd been kneeling.

But the pain was nothing to what it had been, and she smiled as she held out her hand in greeting. Then, as she looked at his face and realised there was a problem, her smile broadened. She wiped her hands on the seat of her overalls and tried again.

'Susie Douglas would be me,' she told him, gripping his reluctant hand and shaking. 'Hi.'

'Hi,' he said, and looked at his hand.

'It's almost clean,' she told him, letting a trace of indignation enter her voice as she realised what he was looking at. 'And it's good, clean dirt. Only a trace wormy.'

'Wormy?'

'Earthworms,' she said, exasperated. This wasn't looking good in terms of long-term relationship. In terms of long-term caring for this garden. 'Worms that make pumpkins grow as big as Priscilla here. Not the kind that go straight to your liver and grow till they come out your eyeballs.'

'Um…fine.' He was starting to sound confounded.

'I'm transferring them to the compost,' she told him, deciding she'd best be patient. 'I'm laying concrete pavers to the conservatory, and how awful would it be to be an earthworm encased in concrete? Do you want to see the conservatory?'

'Um…sure.'

'I might as well show you while we're out here,' she told him. 'You've inherited all this pile, and the conservatory's brilliant. It was falling into disrepair when I arrived, but I've built it up. It's almost like the old orangeries they have in grand English houses.'

'You're American,' he said on a note of discovery. 'But you're…'

'I'm the castle relic,' she told him. 'Hang on a minute. I need to check something.'

She limped across to the closest window, hoisted herself up and peered through to where Rose snoozed in her cot.

'Nope. Still fine.'

'What's fine?' he asked, more and more bemused.

'Rose. My daughter.' She gestured to the headphones now lying abandoned in the mud. 'You thought I was listening to hip-hop while I worked? I was listening to the sounds of my daughter sleeping. Much more reassuring.' She turning and starting to walk toward the conservatory. 'Relics are what they used to call us in the old days,' she said over her shoulder. 'They're the women left behind when their lords died.'

'And your lord was…'

'Rory,' she told him. 'Your cousin. He was Scottish-Australian but he met me in the States.'

'I don't know anything about my cousins.' She was limping toward a glass-panelled building on the north side of the house, moving so fast he had to lengthen his stride to keep up with her.

'You don't know anything about the family?'

'I didn't know anyone existed until I got the lawyer's letter.'

'Saying you were an earl.' She chuckled. 'How

cool. It's like Cinderella. You should have been destitute, living in a garret.' She glanced over her shoulder, eyeing him appraisingly. 'But they tell me you're some sort of financier in Manhattan. I guess you weren't in any garret.'

'It was a pretty upmarket garret,' he admitted. They reached the conservatory doors, and she swung them wide so he could appreciate the vista. 'Wow!'

'It is wow,' she said, approving.

It certainly was. The conservatory was as big as three or four huge living rooms and it was almost thirty feet high. It looked almost a cathedral, he thought, dazed. The beams were vast and blackened with glass panels set between. Hundreds of glass panels.

'The beams came from St Mary's Cathedral just south of Sydney,' Susie told him. 'St Mary's burned down just after the war when Angus was building this place. He couldn't resist. He had all the usable timbers trucked here. For the last few years he didn't have enough energy to keep it up, but since I've been here I've been restoring it. I love it.'

He knew she did. He could hear it in her voice.

She didn't look like any relic he'd met before.

Susie was wearing men's overalls, liberally dirt-stained. She was shortish, slim, with an open, friendly face. She had clear, brown enquiring eyes, and her auburn curls were caught back in a ponytail that threatened to unravel at any minute. A long white scar ran across her forehead—hardly noticeable except that it accentuated the lines of strain around her eyes. She was still young but her face had seen…life?

Her husband had been murdered, he remembered. That's what the lawyers had told him. Back in New York it had seemed a fantastic tale but suddenly it was real. Bleakly real.

'Do you know about the family?' she asked, as if she'd guessed his thoughts and knew he needed an explanation.

'Very little,' he told her. 'I'd like to hear more. Angus was the last earl. He died childless. Your husband, Rory, was his eldest nephew, and he and the second nephew, Kenneth, are both dead. I'm the youngest nephew. I never knew Angus, I certainly didn't know about the title, and I'm still trying to figure things out. Am I right so far?'

'Pretty much.'

'Angus and my father and another brother— Rory and Kenneth's father—left Scotland just after the war?'

'Apparently the family castle was a dark and gloomy pile on the west coast of Scotland,' she told him. 'The castle was hit by an incendiary bomb during the war and it burned to the ground. As far as I can gather, no one grieved very much. The boys had been brought up in an atmosphere that was almost poisonous. Angus inherited everything, the others nothing, and the estate was entailed in such a way that he couldn't do anything about it. After the fire they decided to leave. Angus said your father was the first to go. He boarded a boat to America and Angus never heard from him again.'

'And Angus and…what was the other brother called—David?'

'Angus was in the air force and he was injured toward the end of the war. While he was recuperating he met Deirdre. She was a nurse and her family had been killed in the London Blitz, so when he was discharged they decided to make their home in Australia. David followed.' She hesitated. 'The relationship was hard, and the resentment followed through to the sons.'

'I don't understand.'

'A situation where the eldest son gets everything and others get nothing is asking for trouble.' She walked forward and lifted a ripening cumquat into her hands. She touched it gently and then let it go again, releasing it so it swung on its branch like a beautiful mobile. There were hundreds of cumquats, Hamish thought, still dazzled by the beauty of the place.

Did one eat cumquats? He'd only ever seen them as decorator items in the foyers of five-star hotels.

'Angus rebuilt his castle here,' she said. 'It was a mad thing to do, but it gave the men of this town a job when things were desperate. Maybe it wasn't as crazy as it sounds. He and Deirdre didn't have children but David had two. Rory and Kenneth. I married Rory.'

'They told me that Kenneth murdered Rory,' he said flatly. It had to be talked about, he decided, so why not now?

She pushed her cumquat so it swung again and something in her face tightened, but she didn't falter from answering. 'There was such hate,' she said softly. 'Angus said his brothers hated him from the start, and Kenneth obviously felt the same about Rory. Rory travelled to the States to get away from it. He met me and he didn't even tell me about the family fortune. But, of course, it was still entailed. Rory was still going to inherit and Kenneth wanted it. Enough...enough to kill. Then, when he was... found out...he killed himself.'

'Which is where I come in,' he said softly, trying to deflect the anguish she couldn't disguise.

She took a deep breath. 'Which is where you come in,' she said and turned to face him. 'Welcome to Loganaich Castle, my lord,' she said simply. 'I hope you'll deal with your inheritance with Angus's dignity. And I hope the hate stops now.'

'I hope you'll help me.'

'I'm going home,' she told him. 'I've had enough of…of whatever is here. It's your inheritance. Rory and Angus have left me enough money to keep me more than comfortable. I'm leaving you to it.'

CHAPTER TWO

THIS was where he took over, Hamish thought. This was where he said, *Thank you very much, can I have the keys?*

The whole thing was preposterous. He should never have let Jodie insinuate her crazy ideas into his mind.

The thought of being left alone with his very own castle was almost scary.

'Let's not do anything hasty,' he told Susie. 'I'll get a bed for the night in town, and we'll sit down and work things out in the morning.'

'You're not staying here?' she asked, startled.

'This has been your home,' he said. 'I'm not kicking you out.'

'We do have fourteen bedrooms.'

He hesitated. 'How do you know I'm not like Kenneth?'

She met his gaze and held. 'You're not like Kenneth. I can see.' She bit her lip and turned back to concentrate on her cumquat. 'Bitterness leaves its mark.'

'It's not fair that I inherit—'

'Angus and Rory between them left me all I need, thank you very much,' she said, and there was now a trace of anger in her voice. 'No one owes me anything. I'm not due for anything, and I don't care about fairness or unfairness in terms of inheritance. Thinking like that has to stop. I have a profession and I'll return to it. To kill for money…'

'But if your baby had been a boy he would have inherited,' he said softly. 'It's unjust.'

'You think that bothers me?'

'I'm sure it doesn't.'

'Fine,' she said flatly. 'So that's settled. You needn't worry. The escutcheon is firmly fixed in the male line, so there's no point in me stabbing you in the middle of the night or putting arsenic in your porridge.'

'Toast,' he said. 'I don't eat porridge.'

She blinked. This conversation was crazy.

But maybe that was the way to go. She'd had enough of being serious. 'You don't eat porridge?' she demanded, mock horrified. 'What sort of a laird are you?'

'I'm not a laird.'

'Oh, yes, you are,' she said, starting to smile. 'Or you probably are. Fancy clothes or not, you have definite laird potential.'

'I thought I was an earl?'

'You're that, too,' she told him. 'And of course you'll stay that as long as you live. But being laird is a much bigger responsibility.'

'I don't even know what a laird is.'

'The term's not used so much any more,' she said. 'It means a landed proprietor. But it's more than that. It's one who holds the dignity of an estate. Angus was absolutely a laird. I'm not sure what sort of laird Rory would have made. Kenneth would never have been one. But you, Hamish Douglas? Will you make a laird?'

'That sounds like a challenge,' he said, and she jutted her chin a little and met his look head on.

'Maybe it is.'

He hesitated, not sure where to take this. Not at all sure that she wasn't just a little crazy herself. 'Maybe I'd best stay in town,' he said. 'I'll come back in the morning to organise things.'

'There's not much to organise,' she told him. 'But you need to stay here. There's only the Black Stump pub, and Thursday is darts night. There's no sleep to be had in the Black Stump before three in the morning. Anyway, if anyone moves out it should be me. It's your home now. Not mine.'

'But you will stay,' he said urgently. 'I need to learn about the place.'

'What do you intend to do with it?'

There was only one answer to that. 'Sell.'

Her face stilled. 'Can you do that?'

'I've checked.' Actually, Marcia had checked. 'If I put the money into trust, then, yes.' The capital needed to stay intact but the interest alone—plus the rent rolls from the land in Scotland—would keep him wealthy even without his own money.

'You don't need me to help you sell it,' she snapped, and then bit her lip. 'I'm sorry. I know selling seems sensible but…but…'

She took a deep breath, and suddenly her voice was laced with emotion—and pain. 'I'll stay tonight. Tomorrow I'll pack and go stay with my sister until I can arrange a flight home.'

'Susie, there's no need—'

'There is a need,' she said, and suddenly her voice sounded almost desperate.

'But why?'

'Because I keep falling in love,' she snapped, the desperation intensifying. 'I fell so far into love with Rory that his death broke my heart. I fell for Angus. And now I've fallen for your stupid castle, for your dumb suits of armour—they're called Eric and Ernst, by the way, and they like people chatting to them—for your stupid compost system, which is second to none in the entire history of the western world—I've even fallen for your worms. I keep breaking my heart and I'm not going to do it any more. I'm going home to the States and I'm going back to landscape gardening and Rose and I are going to live happily ever after. Now, if you'll excuse me, I need to finish my work. Bring your gear in. You can have any bedroom you like upstairs. The whole top floor is yours. Rose and I are downstairs. But I need to do some fast digging before Rose wakes from her nap. Dinner's at seven and there's plenty to spare. I'll see you in the kitchen.'

And without another word she brushed past him, out of the conservatory and back into the brilliant autumn sunshine. She grabbed her spade she'd left leaning against the fence and headed off the way they'd come. Her back was stiff and set—her spade was over her shoulder like a soldier carrying a gun—she looked the picture of determination.

But he wasn't fooled.

He'd seen the glimmer of unshed tears as she'd turned away—and as she reached the garden gate she started, stiffly, to run.

'Kirsty, he's here. The new owner.'

Susie had been crying. Kirsty could hear it in her voice, and her heart stilled.

'Sweetheart, is he horrid? Is he another Kenneth? I'll be right there.'

'I don't need you to come.' There was an audible sniff.

'Then what's wrong?'

'He's going to sell.'

Susie's sister paused. She'd known this would happen. It was inevitable. But somehow…somehow she'd hoped…

Susie had come so far. Dreadfully injured in the engineered car crash which had killed her husband, Susie had drifted into a depression so deep it had been almost crippling. But with this place, with her love for the old earl, with her love for the wonderful castle garden and her enchantment with her baby daughter, she'd been hauled back from the brink. For the last few months she'd been back to the old Susie, laughing, bossy, full of plans…

Angus's death had been expected, a peaceful end to a long and happy life, but Kirsty knew that her twin hadn't accepted it yet. Hadn't moved on.

Kirsty was a doctor, and she'd seen this before. Loving and caring for someone to the end, watching them fade but never really coming to terms with the reality that the end meant the end.

'So…' she said at last, cautiously, and Susie hiccuped back a sob.

'I'm going home. Back to the States. Tomorrow.'

'Um… I suspect you won't be able to get travel papers for Rose by tomorrow.'

'I have a passport for her already. There are only a couple of last-minute documents I need to organise. Can I come and stay with you and Jake until then?'

'Sure,' Kirsty said uneasily, mentally organising her house to accommodate guests. They were extending the back of the house to make a bigger bedroom for the twins—and for the new little one she hadn't quite got round to telling her sister about—but they'd squash in somehow. 'But why? What's he like?'

'He's gorgeous.'

Silence.

'I…see.' Kirsty turned thoughtful. 'So why do you want to come and stay at our house? Don't you trust yourself?'

'It's not like that.'

'No?'

'No,' Susie snapped. 'It's just… He's not like Rory and he's not like Angus and I can't bear him to be here. Just—owning everything. He doesn't even know about compost. I said we had the best compost system in the world and he looked at me like I was talking Swahili.'

'Normal, in fact.'

'He's not normal. He wears cream suede shoes.'

'Right.'

'Don't laugh at me, Kirsty Cameron.'

'When have I ever laughed at you?'

'All the time. Can I come and stay?'

'Not tonight. Tomorrow I'll air one of the new rooms and see if I can get the paint fumes out. You can surely bear to stay with him one night. Or… would you like me to come and stay with you?'

'No. I mean…well, he offered to stay at the pub so he must be safe enough. I said he could stay.'

'Would you like to borrow Boris?'

'Fat lot of good Boris would be as a guard dog.'

'He's looked after us before,' Kirsty said with dignity. OK, Boris was a lanky, misbred, over-boisterous dog, but he'd proved a godsend in the past.

Faint laughter returned to her sister's voice at that. 'He did. He's wonderful. But I'm fine. I'll feed Lord Hamish Douglas and give him a bed tonight and then I'll leave him to his own devices.' The smile died from her words. 'Oh, but, Kirsty, to see him sell the castle…I don't see how I can bear it.'

The castle was stunning.

While Susie finished her gardening Hamish took the opportunity to explore. And he was stunned.

It was an amazing, over-the-top mixture of grandeur and kitsch. The old earl hadn't stinted when it came to building a castle as a castle ought to be built—to last five hundred years or more. But into his grand building he'd put furnishings that were anything but grand. Hamish had an Aunt Molly who'd love this stuff. He thought of Molly as he winced at the truly horrible plastic chandeliers hung along the passageways, at the plastic plants in plastic urns, at the cheap gilt Louis XIV tables and chairs, and at the settees with bright gold crocodile legs. It was so awful it was brilliant.

Then he opened the bathroom door and Queen Victoria gazed down at him in blatant disapproval from behind an aspidistra. He burst out laughing but he closed the door fast. A man couldn't do what a man had to do under that gaze. He'd have to find another bathroom or head to the pub.

More exploring.

He found another bathroom, this one fitted with a chandelier so large it almost edged out the door. The portrait here was of Henry the Eighth. OK. He could live with Henry. He found five empty bedrooms and chose one with a vast four-poster bed and a view of the ocean that took his breath away.

He decided staying here was possible.

Susie was still digging in the garden below. He watched her for a minute—and went back to thinking. Staying here was fraught with difficulties.

What had she said? She'd fallen in love with a

castle, a compost bin, the worms she was digging out of the mud right now.

She'd cried.

The set look of her shoulders said she might still be crying.

He didn't do tears.

The smile he'd had on his face since he'd met Queen Victoria faded. He put Susie's emotion carefully away from him.

He sorted his gear, hanging shirts neatly, jackets neatly, lining up shoes. He had enough clothes to last him a week. Otherwise he'd have to find a laundry.

Marcia called him a control freak. Marcia was right.

Almost involuntarily, he crossed to the window again. Susie was digging with almost ferocious intensity, taking out her pain on the mud. He saw her pause and wipe her overalled arm across her eyes.

She was crying.

He should stay at the pub. Darts or not.

That was dumb. Fleeing emotion? What sort of laird did that make him?

He owned this pile. He was Lord Hamish Douglas. Ridiculous! If his mother knew what was happening she'd cry, too, he thought, and then winced.

Too many tears!

For the first part of his life tears had been all he'd known. When he'd been three his father had suicided. That was his first memory. Too many women, too many tears, endless sobbing…

The tears hadn't stopped. His mother had held her husband's death to her heart—over his head—for the rest of her life. She held it still.

Her voice came back to him in all its pathos.

'Wash your knees, Hamish. Your father would hate it if he saw his son with grubby knees. Oh, I can't bear it that he can't be here to see.'

Tears.

'Do your homework, Hamish. Oh, if you fail…'

Tears.

Or, as he'd shown no signs of failing, 'Your father would be so proud…' And the sobbing would continue. Endlessly. His mother, her friends, his aunts.

There'd been tears every day of his life until he'd broken away, fiercely, among floods of recriminations—and more tears—and made his own life. He'd taken a job in Manhattan, far away from his Californian home. Far from the tears.

He hated the crying—the endless emotion. Hated it! His job now was an oasis of calm, where emotions were the last thing he needed. Marcia was cool, calm and self-contained. Nary a tear. That was his life.

He shouldn't have come, he thought. This title thing was ridiculous. He'd never use it. Marcia thought it was great and if she wanted to use the 'Lady' bit then that was fine by him.

Marcia would never cry.

He'd call her, he decided, retrieving his cell phone. Manhattan was sixteen hours behind here. Four in the afternoon here made it midnight back home. Marcia would be in bed, reading the long-winded legal briefs she read as avidly as some read crime novels.

She answered on the first ring. 'Hamish. Fabulous. You're there, then. Should I address you as Lord Douglas?'

'Cut it out, Marcia,' he said uncomfortably, and she backed off in an instant. That was the great thing about Marcia. She never intruded on his personal space.

'I'm sorry. Did you have a good journey?'

'Fine, thank you.'

There was a moment's pause. Marcia was expecting him to say something else, he knew, but he was still watching Susie under his window. Susie was digging as if her life depended on it.

'What's it like?' Marcia said eventually, all patience. 'The castle?'

'Crazy. Queen Victoria's in my bathroom.'

'Who?'

'Queen Vic. It's OK. I've changed to one with Henry the Eighth.'

'What are you talking about?'

'Portraits in the bathroom. The place is full of kitsch. Queen Victoria is a trifle...distracting.'

'Oh.' She sounded annoyed. 'For heaven's sake, Hamish, just take it down.'

That'd be sensible, he thought. He'd take all the portraits down. He'd send them to his Aunty Molly. As soon as Susie left.

'Was there anyone there to meet you?'

'Rory Douglas's widow. The lawyer told us about Rory Douglas.'

'He did,' she said, and he could hear her leafing through documents till she found what she wanted. 'I've got the letter here. He was murdered by his brother, which is why you inherited. What's she like?'

'Emotional.'

'A lachrymose widow,' she said with instant sympathy. 'My poor Hamish, how awful. Will she be hard to move?'

'What do you mean?'

'If she's been living there...she's not a tenant for life or anything, is she? You can still sell?'

'She offered to move out tonight.'

'That's great!'

'I can hardly kick her out tonight,' he said and heard her regroup.

'Well, of course not. Will you need to use some

of the inheritance to resettle her, do you think? Does she have somewhere to go?'

'She's American. She's coming home.'

'Not entirely silly, then,' Marcia said with approval. 'She has plans. What about you? How long do you think it'll take to put the place on the market?'

'I'll paint a "For Sale" sign on the gate tomorrow.'

'Be serious,' she told him. 'Hamish, this is a lot of money. If the place is full of kitsch you'd best clean it out so it doesn't put potential buyers off. Will it sell as a potential hotel?'

That much he knew. 'Yes.'

'Then there are specialist realtors. International hotel dealers. I'll get back to you with names.'

'Fine.'

Was it fine?

Of course it was fine. What Marcia suggested was sensible.

He thought about posting Queen Victoria to his Aunt Molly.

He watched Susie.

'Steak and chips.'

Hamish had only partly opened the kitchen door when Susie's voice announced the menu. He blinked, gazing around the room in something approaching awe. This room was built to feed an army.

It had huge overhead beams, a wonderful flagstoned floor, an efficient gas range, as well as an old-fashioned slow combustion stove.

'How do you like your steak?' she demanded.

She was being brisk. She wasn't crying. Emotion had been put on the backburner, and she was being fiercely efficient.

'Medium rare,' he said, and she smiled.

'Great.' Then her smile faded, just a little. 'Medium rare, eh?'

'Is that a problem?'

'It might be,' she said cautiously. 'It depends.'

'On what?'

'On how it turns out. I was planning on beans on toast before you arrived. Much more dependable.'

'You know where you are with a bean,' he agreed, and she looked at him with suspicion.

'Don't you give me a hard time. Kirsty's bad enough.'

'Kirsty?'

'My sister. She and her husband are the local doctors. Kirsty said I have to give you something good to celebrate your first night here. She dropped off the steaks a few minutes ago. She would have stayed to meet you but she has evening clinic and was in a rush. But she left Boris, just in case you turn nasty.'

Boris was—apparently—a nondescript, brownish

dog of the Heinz variety who was currently lying under a high chair. A toddler—a little girl about a year old—was waving a rusk above the dog's head, and the dog had immolated himself, upside down, all legs in the air, waiting with eternal patience for the rusk to drop.

The dog hadn't so much as looked up as Hamish had entered. Every fibre of his being was tuned to the rusk. Some guard dog!

'What will Boris do if I turn nasty?' he asked, and Susie grinned.

'He'll think of something. He's a very resourceful dog.' She produced a frying-pan and then looked doubtfully at the steaks.

The steaks lay in all their glory on a plate by the stove. They looked magnificent.

'How are you planning on cooking them?' Hamish asked.

'I'll fry them,' she said with a vague attempt at confidence. 'That doesn't sound too difficult.'

'You're cooking chips?'

'They're oven fries,' she confessed. 'Kirsty brought them as well. You put them in the oven, you set the timer for twenty minutes and you take them out again. Even I can't mess that up. Probably.'

She was making a huge effort to be cheerful, he thought, and he'd try to join her.

'Tell me you're not responsible for Queen Victoria,' he said and she grinned. She had a great grin, he thought. He was reminded suddenly of Jodie.

Jodie would love Loganaich Castle.

'Aunty Deirdre is responsible for Queen Vic,' Susie told him. 'Angus gave her carte blanche to decorate the castle as she saw fit—but he also gave her a very small budget. I think she did great.'

'She surely did,' he said faintly. Susie brushed past him on her way to the fridge and he started feeling even more disoriented. She'd showered since he'd last seen her. Or since he'd last smelt her. She was wearing clean jeans and a soft pink T-shirt, tucked in. Her hair was still in a ponytail but it was almost controlled now. And she smelt like citrus. Fresh and lemony. Nice.

'Mama,' the little girl said. 'Mama.'

'Sweetheart,' Susie said, and that was enough to slam reality home. His mother always called him 'sweetheart' when she was trying to manipulate him.

He stopped thinking how nice she smelt, and thought instead how great it was that he had his Marcia and his whole life controlled, and he'd never have to cope with this sort of messy tearful existence.

Susie was carrying a tub of dripping to the stove. She scooped out a tablespoon or more into the frying pan. Then looked at it. Dubiously.

'What are you doing?' he said faintly, and she raised her eyebrows as if he'd said something stupid.

'Cooking.'

'Deep frying or shallow frying?'

'Is there a difference?

He sighed. 'Yes. But with that amount of fat in the pan you're doing neither. The chips are already in the oven?'

'Yes.'

'How long have they been in?'

'Five minutes.'

'How do you have your steak?'

'Any way I can get it.'

'Then you'll have it medium rare as well, and I have five minutes before I start cooking. Can you find me an apron?'

'You're kidding.'

'No.'

'Gee,' she said, stunned, but willing not only to hand over cooking but to be admiring while she was at it. 'You really can cook?'

'I can cook steak.'

'Would you like to make a salad, too?' Her voice said she knew she was pushing her luck. It was almost teasing. 'I can mix up chopped lettuce and tomato but anything else is problematic.'

He sighed. 'I can make a salad. But I do need an apron.'

'An apron,' she said, as if she'd never heard of such a thing.

'Something to cover—'

'I know what an apron is,' she said with dignity. She looked down at her faded, work-worn clothes. 'I just never use one. But I'll bet that Deirdre was an apron lady.'

She turned and searched a capacious drawer by the door. 'Hey!' She held up something that took Hamish's breath away. Bright pink with purple roses, bib and skirt, the garment had flounces all round the edge and a huge pink ribbon at the back. 'Good old Deirdre,' Susie said in satisfaction. 'I knew she wouldn't let me down. You'll look great in this.'

Yeah, right. He could just see the next front page of the *Financial Review*. There were guys back home who'd kill to see this, and he was well known enough to hit the social pages of the tabloids.

He eyed Susie in suspicion. Mobile phones could also be cameras. If you wore an apron like this, you trusted no one.

'You have a washing machine?' he demanded, trying not to sound desperate.

'I have a washing machine.'

'Then I'll make do without the apron.' Some things were no-brainers. 'Just this once.'

'That's big of you,' she told him, laying the frills aside with regret. 'Why are you tipping out the dripping?'

'That was half an inch of fat, and if you thing I'm spoiling my first Australian steak, you have another think coming.'

'Ooh,' she said in mock admiration. 'Bossy as well as a good cook.'

'Watch your fries,' he told her, disconcerted.

'Hey, we'll get on fine,' she said happily. 'You can cook. I can't. A marriage made in heaven.'

Then she realised what she'd said and she blushed. The blush started from her eyes and moved out, and he thought, She's lovely. She's just gorgeous.

Rose chortled from her high chair and Hamish allowed himself to be distracted. He needed to be distracted. Whew!

Rose was a chubby toddler, dressed only in a nappy and a grubby T-shirt reading MY AUNTY WENT TO NEW YORK AND ALL SHE BROUGHT ME WAS ONE LOUSY T-SHIRT. She had flame-coloured curls, just like her mother, and huge green eyes that gazed at him as if expecting to be vastly entertained.

It was very disconcerting to be gazed at like that. He'd never been gazed at like that.

In truth, Hamish had never met a toddler.

This situation was getting out of hand.

Rosie chortled again, raised her hand and lifted her rusk. It fell. On the floor beneath, on his back, Boris did a fast, curving slide so his mouth was right where it needed to be. The rusk disappeared without a trace.

Rose and her mother—and Hamish—all gazed at Boris. Boris gazed back up at Rose in adoration, and then opened his mouth wide again.

Hamish laughed.

Susie stared.

'What?' he said, disconcerted, and she flushed and turned away.

'N-nothing.'

'Something.'

'It's just… For a minute…' She took a deep breath. 'The Douglas men,' she said. 'Angus and Rory had the same laugh. Low and rumbly and nice. And it's here again. In this kitchen. Where it belongs.'

For a moment neither of them spoke. Did she know what power she had to move him? he wondered.

He'd never known his father. Oh, he had a vague memory of someone being there, a grey, silent, ghost-like presence, but that was all. He'd seen faded photographs of a man who didn't look like him. He had no connection at all.

And suddenly he did.

He didn't do emotion.

'I'm hardly a Douglas,' he said, more sharply than he'd intended. 'My father died when I was three, and I've had no contact with anyone but my mother's family.'

'But you *are* a Douglas.'

'In name only.'

'You don't want to be a Douglas?'

Not if it means all this emotion, he thought, but he didn't say it.

'Move over,' he told her instead. 'It's time to put the steak on. Four minutes either side, which gives me time to whip up a salad. But there's no time for idle chat.'

'You don't do idle chat?'

'No.'

'I'll concentrate on my chips, then,' she told him, and proceeded to sit on the floor, flick on the oven light and watch. Which was distracting all on its own. 'I know when to butt out where I'm not wanted.'

'I didn't mean to be rude.'

'Neither did I,' she told him. 'But maybe that's the way we have to be. You don't want to be a Douglas. I can't bear to be near one. So let's get tonight over with and then we can both move on in the direction we intend to go.'

CHAPTER THREE

SHE woke to singing.

She must be dreaming, she decided, and closed her eyes but a moment later she opened them again.

"'I'll be true to the song I sing. And live and die a pirate king.'"

It was a rich, deep baritone, wafting in from the window out to the garden. Straight out of Gilbert and Sullivan.

Hamish?

It was early. Too early. She'd had trouble getting to sleep. Rosie was still soundly sleeping and she didn't have to get up yet. She didn't want to get up yet.

She closed her eyes.

"'It is, it is a glorious thing, to be a pirate king.'"

She opened one eye and looked at her clock.

Six a.m.

The man was mad, she decided. Singing in the vegetable garden at six in the morning.

It was a great voice.

OK, she'd just look. She rolled out of bed, crawled across the floor under the level of the sill, then raised herself cautiously so she was just peeking…

He was digging her path. *Her* path!

The window was open and the curtains were drawn. Before she'd even thought logically, she'd shoved her hands on the sill and swung herself out. 'What do you think you're doing?'

Hamish paused in mid-dig. He was wearing shorts. And boots.

Nothing else.

This wasn't a stockbroker's body, Susie thought as he set down his spade and decided what to say. The man had a serious six-pack. He was tanned and muscled—as if he'd spent half his life on a farm rather than in a stockbroker's office.

He had great legs.

Oh, for heaven's sake…

'Whose boots are they?' she demanded, and then thought, What a ridiculous question to ask. But the boots were decrepit—surely not carefully brought over from New York.

'I found them in the wet room,' he told her, looking like he was trying not smile. 'There's a whole pile. I figured if I inherited the castle with contents included, then at least one lot of boots must be mine. They're a size or two big but I'm wearing two pairs of socks. What do you think? Will I take Manhattan by storm?' He raised a knee to hold up a boot for inspection.

Boris had been supervising the path-digging lying down. Now the big dog rose, put out a tongue and licked the specified boot. Just tasting…

It was such a ridiculous statement—such a ridiculous situation—that Susie started to giggle.

Then she suddenly thought about what she was wearing and stopped giggling. Maybe she should hop right back in through the window.

But he'd already noticed. 'Nice elephants,' he said politely.

And she thought, Yep, the window was a good idea. She was wearing a pair of short—very short— boxer-type pyjama bottoms and a top that matched. Purple satin with yellow and crimson elephants.

There was a story behind these elephants. Susie's two little step-nieces had wanted pyjamas with elephants on them. Harriet from the post office had been in Sydney for a week to visit an ailing sister and had thus been commissioned to find pyjama material with elephants. What she'd found had been royal purple satin with yellow and red elephants— the lot going much cheaper by the roll. Harriet had been so pleased that she'd bought the entire roll, and every second person in Dolphin Bay was now sporting elephant-covered nightwear.

'They're home-made,' Susie managed. 'I know the seamstress.' She managed a smile and Hamish thought—not for the first time—what a lovely smile she had. 'She'll make you some too if you like.'

'No, thank you,' he said hurriedly, and she grinned.

'You could really take New York by storm with these.'

'I don't think Manhattan is ready for those pyjamas.'

There was a silence. She was trying not to look at his six-pack. He looked like he was trying not to look at her pyjamas.

'What are you doing?' she asked, as much to break the silence as anything. Though it was obvious.

The garden was in the full fruit of late autumn. The fruit trees were laden. The lavender hedge was alive with early-morning bees, everything was neat and shipshape, and the only discordant note was the path she'd started digging. She'd dug the first twenty yards. Twenty yards had taken her two days.

Hamish had dug another fifteen.

'I assume you wanted the rest dug,' he told her. She bit her lip. 'I did. It's just…'

'I've put the soil in the compost area,' he told her, guessing her qualms. 'I've left it separate so you can mix it as you want.'

One question answered.

'And the worms are in the yellow bucket,' he told her, answering her second.

He was laughing at her! He'd done what represented over a day's work. She should be grateful. She was grateful! But he was laughing.

'Worms are important,' she said defensively, and he nodded.

'I've always thought so. But not the kind that come out of your eyeballs.'

'There's no need to mock.'

'I'm not mocking.'

More silence.

'You don't get muscles like those sitting behind a desk,' she said tentatively. She felt she shouldn't mention those muscles—but she was unable to stop looking at them.

'I work out.'

'You use a gym?'

'There's a gym in the building where I live.'

Of course. More silence while she tried again not to concentrate on muscles.

Oh, OK, she'd look. Guys looked at good-looking women all the time. She could do a little payback.

'So I'm not doing the wrong thing?' he prompted when the silence got a bit stretched—and she hauled her thoughts together and tried to think what she ought to be saying. What she should be looking at.

'Of—of course you're not. I'm very grateful.'

'What are you planning on doing once you've dug?'

'I have a pile of pavers under the lemon tree.' She pointed. 'There.'

He looked. And winced. 'They look like they weigh a ton. You were going to lay them yourself?'

'Of course I was.'

'But you've been injured,' he said. 'The lawyer told me—'

'I'm fine.'

'You limp.'

'I don't limp much. I'm fine.' She took a deep breath, moving on. 'Not that it matters. They're your pavers now.'

'Susie, do you have to leave so soon?'

'I…'

'I'm here for three weeks,' he said urgently. 'I had a phone call this morning from the States. That's why I'm up early. A combination of jet-lag and a phone call at four. The best way to sell this place—'

Do I want to hear this? Susie thought, but she hardly had a choice.

'—is via a realtor who specialises in selling exclusive country hotels. He comes, assesses potential, and if he likes what he sees then he'll put this place on his list of vendors and promote the place inter-nationally. He'll be in Australia next week. Marcia thinks I should persuade you to stay till then.'

Marcia? Susie wondered, but she didn't ask.

'Why do you want me to stay?'

'You know the history of the place. The agent holds that important. If people come to an exclusive location they want the personal touch. They'll want to know about Angus and the family and the castle back in Scotland. All its history.'

'I'll write it out for you.'

'I'll sell the place for more if you're here to give a guided tour,' Hamish said flatly. 'Widow of the in-cumbent earl's heir…'

'If you think you're going to play on Rory's murder to get your *atmosphere*—'

'I didn't say that.'

'You didn't need to,' she told him, and glowered. 'But will you stay? I'll pay you.'

'Why will you pay me?'

'Well…' He considered. 'You could still pave the garden.' He eyed her, assessing and guessing her weakness. 'You would like to get this path finished.'

'I would,' she admitted, and bit her lip.

'Then I'm happy to pay landscape gardening hourly rates. Think about it,' he said—and went right back to digging. Leaving her to think about it.

Which slightly discomposed her. She'd expected more…argument?

Staying on here was dumb, she thought. More than dumb. She looked at Hamish's broad, bare back and she thought that staying could be unsettling. Would be unsettling. She hadn't looked at another man since Rory had died and, of course, she never would, but there was that about Hamish which made her very solid foundations seem just a little shaky round the edges.

She didn't want her foundations shaken. Her world had been shaken quite enough for one lifetime.

So she should go. Immediately.

But then…

She and Rose had lived here for over a year. She'd started packing after Angus had died, but her efforts had been desultory to say the least. She needed to get organised. Today's deadline might not be actually feasible.

She thought about it for a bit more. She watched Hamish dig some more. He'd have blisters, she decided, seeing him almost inconspicuously shift the spade in his hands. She knew what he was doing. She'd done it herself often and often. He was finding unblistered skin to work with.

He was strong and willing but he wasn't accustomed to this sort of work. He was a Manhattan money-maker.

The locals would hate the idea of the new laird being such a man.

But that started more ideas forming. Hamish was asking a favour of her. Maybe she could ask one of him. Angus's death had left such a void. Maybe they could have a laird one last time, she thought. Maybe…

'I'll do it, but not for payment,' she called out, and he looked up, surprised, as if he hadn't expected to see her still to be there.

'You'll stay?'

'Yes.' She grinned. 'I'll even cook.'

'More fries?'

'I can do toast, too. And porridge if you're game.'

He smiled at that, and she thought, Yep, there it was again. The Douglas chuckle and the Douglas smile in a body that wasn't a Douglas body at all. It was a body she knew nothing about and wanted to know nothing about.

She had to get those foundations steady.

'I look forward to meeting your toast, but not your porridge, Mrs Douglas,' he told her formally, and she managed to smile back and then thought maybe smiling wasn't such a good idea. He didn't have enough clothes on. She didn't have enough clothes on. It was too early in the morning.

He was a Douglas!

'Tomorrow's the Dolphin Bay Harvest Thanks-giving fête,' she told him as he started digging again. 'We need a laird.'

'Pardon?' He bent to separate some worms and then dug a couple more spadefuls.

'The laird opens the fête. It's traditional. No one's doing it tomorrow because everyone's still mourning Angus. But not having anyone there will be awful. Maybe we should do it in stages. Maybe we could use you tomorrow as the last of the Douglases.'

His spade paused in mid air—and then kept digging. 'You know, I might not be the last of the Douglases,' he said cautiously. 'The Douglas clan appear to be quite prolific. In fact, if I give you the phone book you might find almost as many Douglases as Smiths, Greens and Nguyens.'

'No, but as far as I know you're the only Lord Douglas in this neck of the woods.'

'Which leaves me…where?'

'Opening the fête tomorrow.'

Another pause in the digging. Another resumption. 'Which involves what exactly?'

'Saying a few words. Just "I now declare this fête open". After the bagpipes stop.'

'Bagpipes,' he said, even more cautiously, and

Susie thought the man wasn't as silly as he looked. Actually, he didn't look the least bit silly.

And he'd guessed where she was headed. She could see the suspicion growing and she almost giggled.

'It's a very nice kilt,' she said.

He set down his spade and turned to her in all seriousness.

'Don't ask it of me, Susie. I have knobbly knees.'

She did giggle then. 'I can see them from here. They're very nice knees.'

'I only show them to other Douglases.'

'Me, you mean.'

'You and my mother.'

'Not…Marcia?'

'Marcia has the sense not to look,' he told her. 'I'd never have exposed them to you but you woke unreasonably early. Normally I have huge signs out. CAUTION: EXPOSED KNEES. So that lets me out of fête opening.'

'Then I'm off to pack.'

'Susie, this is a business trip,' he said, and there was suddenly more than a trace of desperation in his voice. 'I'm not an earl. I'm not Lord Douglas. In this day and age it doesn't make any sense. I won't use the title. I'll sell the castle and I'll get back to my ordinary life.'

'You sound afraid,' she said, and he cast her a look that said she wasn't far off the mark.

'That's dumb. Why would I be afraid?'

'It's not so scary, standing in a kilt and saying a few words.'

'People will expect—'

'They'll expect nothing,' she said softly. 'The people here loved Uncle Angus. He was their laird. You won't know the story but this castle saved the town. After the war the men depended on the schools of couta to make their living—great long fish you catch by trawling in relatively shallow water. But some disease—worms, actually—hit the couta, and the men didn't have boats big enough for deep-sea fishing. Everyone was starting to leave. It was either leave or starve. But then along came Angus. He saw this place, fell in love with it and realised the only thing that could keep it going was another industry. So he persuaded the guardians of his family trust—your family trust—to let him rebuild his castle here. The men worked on the castle while they gradually rebuilt the fishing fleet. The people here loved Angus to bits and his death has caused real heartache. You wearing a kilt tomorrow—no, it won't bring Angus back, but maybe it'll fill a void that for many may seem unbearable.'

Emotion, Hamish thought. More emotion. But Susie's chin was tilted upward. She was defiant rather than lachrymose, throwing him a dare.

Open a fête…

It was a dumb, emotional thing to do. It had no foundation in logic and he should run a mile.

'Why are you digging my path?' she asked.

'I was bored.'

'What are you going to do until this assessor gets here?'

'I'll go through the castle books.' I'll get rid of some kitsch, he thought, but he didn't say it. Marcia was researching a place where he could hire some decent antiques to make the place look firstclass.

Maybe Queen Vic could stay…

Queen Vic was in a plastic gilt frame. She'd been a cheap print and was a bit frayed around the edges. Keeping Queen Vic would be a dumb, emotional decision and he needed to stay tight here.

'The castle books are in the hands of the executors,' Susie told him. 'Mr O'Shannasy's the local solicitor but his office is always closed Fridays. That means you can't start work until Monday. Which leaves the weekend free for fair opening.'

'I have a path to dig.'

'It's my path,' she said, almost belligerently, and then stopped. 'I mean…'

No emotion. 'It's your path until you leave,' he said hurriedly.

'Which is today unless you open the fête.'

'Why is it so important?'

'I just don't want the stage to be empty.'

'It's a sentimental gesture.'

'What's wrong with that?'

'I'm a businessman.'

'You can be a businessman again when you leave here. Be Lord Douglas for a bit. It's your title. Enjoy it.'

'I would have thought lords enjoy themselves by...I don't know, holding lavish banquets. Driving Lamborghinis.'

'You can have porridge and toast for breakfast. We'll put marmalade on top of the toast, banana on top of the porridge, and call it a banquet. And I'll drive you to the fête in Angus's old Ford. It has four wheels, same as a Lamborghini. What's your problem?'

'I don't have a kilt,' he said, backed against a figurative wall but still fighting.

'No.' Her face grew thoughtful. 'And Angus's would be too small. He was a much shorter man.' She hesitated. He saw the telltale wash of emotion cross her face and he flinched. But she had hold of herself again. 'My husband used to come here often before...before he went overseas and we were married. Angus had a kilt made for him from the family tartan. You're almost the same size.'

Great. He'd go to a fête wearing the kilt of this woman's dead husband.

But she'd read his expression.

'I'm not asking for sympathy here,' she told him, and there was suddenly anger flooding her voice. 'You can stop looking as if you're expecting me to burst into tears and tell you you're just like my Rory.'

'I never…'

He had.

'I don't need you,' she snapped.

'Of course you don't need me.'

'It's just the town…so many of the old people… they'll come tomorrow, and Angus has only been dead for a few weeks, and they'll see the empty stage and it'll stay with them and spoil their fête. If you get up in your kilt and open the thing and wander round for a bit and don't tell people you're selling, just say you're not exactly sure what's happening, then the locals will have a splendid talking point instead of a focus for grief. The fête was threatening to be dismal. You have it in your power to retrieve things.'

'I don't want—'

'You want what's right for the castle,' she snapped. 'You want the best monetary outcome. You told me yourself you can get that if I stay on until the assessor comes. So use your head and not your heart, Hamish Douglas. Where's the sense in refusing?'

She had a point. But…

'I don't think I want to,' he said weakly, and she cast him a look that contained pure triumph. She had him and she knew it.

'I'll go look out the kilt,' she told him. 'You're skinnier than Rory. We may need to adjust it. And quit the digging. You have more blisters than you need already. Breakfast in half an hour?'

'Er…yes.'

'The first of your many banquets here, my lord,' she told him. She grinned—and went to find her lord a kilt.

'He's like a fish out of water.'

Actually, he was in water. Hamish was in the shower. His bathroom was right above Susie's and as she'd dialled her sister's number he'd started singing. The Pirate King was being given another airing, and a good one. 'He's here to make money out of the place,' she told Kirsty. 'He's going to sell. I should hate him but…' She hesitated. 'It's like he's some big New York financier but there's someone else underneath.'

'Someone nice?'

'He sings,' Susie explained, and held the receiver out so Kirsty could hear.

'Um…great,' Kirsty said, back on the line after a

moment's bemused listening. 'There's lots of tes-
tosterone in that there baritone. Are you interested?'

Some questions were dumb. 'Why would I be interested?' Susie demanded. 'Anyway, I'm just
ringing to tell you that you can come and take your
dog back. I'm quite safe. And he's agreed to open
the fête tomorrow.'

'He's agreed…' There was a moment's stunned
silence and then something that sounded like a sniff
from the other end of the line. 'He's opening the
fête? Wearing the Douglas tartan?'

'Wearing the Douglas tartan.'

'Oh, Susie…'

'You won't weep on him, will you?' Susie asked,
becoming nervous, and Kirsty sniffed again.

'No, but everyone else will.'

'They'd better not. He'll run.'

'Once he's opened the fête he can run all he
wants,' Kirsty said directly. 'That empty stage
was going to seem awful. But for the opening to
go to another Douglas… It'll almost seem like a
happy ending.'

'Yeah, well it's not,' Susie said, suddenly breathless. 'Or…well, I guess it is an ending and it's better
than it might be. This'll be something like closure.'

'But he's really nice?' Kirsty demanded, and
Susie flushed. She was Kirsty's twin and she knew

where her sister's thoughts were headed, often before Kirsty did. She knew where they were headed now, and she had no wish to go there.

'My daughter is attempting to climb onto the back of your dog,' she told her sister with what she hoped was dignity. 'I need to go.'

And she replaced the receiver on any more conjecture.

Things were formal at breakfast. Hamish was dressed again as he might dress for a casual stroll down Fifth Avenue. Understated. Expensive. Cool.

Susie had dressed in shorts and a T-shirt which stayed pristine until she gave Rose her first piece of toast and Rose gave it back. She was therefore decorated with a raspberry streak centre front. Not so cool.

No matter. There was a small glitch when Hamish refused porridge. Susie thought this was one of the few things she could cook—and what sort of a Douglas was he if he didn't eat porridge?—but she finally decided magnanimously to overlook it. They ate their toast with only social pleasantries expressed between mouthfuls.

Hamish appeared not to notice Rosie and Boris doing their best to make him laugh. He didn't comment on Susie's raspberry streak. He appeared to have switched into another mode, one where he was polite and courteous but otherwise remote.

Fine. She could handle this, she decided.

A non-porridge-eating Douglas.

They finished eating. Susie wiped off her small daughter. Then, somewhat at a loss, she offered a full tour and her offer was accepted.

This was good, Susie thought as she led the way through the castle. She carried Rose, Boris following behind as she opened room after room and explained the contents. Formality would get them through the next few days. It was only when Hamish stopped being polite and grinned that her insides started doing funny things.

'This is bedroom number seven…'

'I saw this yesterday,' Hamish said politely. 'All by myself.'

'You looked through the bedrooms by yourself?'

'I was choosing one. You told me I could. Any on the first floor.'

'They're your bedrooms,' she said, and flushed. 'Am I boring you?'

'It's a very nice castle.'

'I'm boring you.'

'What about the beach?' he asked. The sea was right out every north-facing window, tantalising with its sapphire shimmer.

'There's a track just over the road,' she told him. 'When the place is turned into a hotel you may need to build an inclinator. It's a bit steep.'

'But the track leads to the beach.'

'Yes.'

'A swimmable beach?'

'Very much so.'

'You're going to offer to show me?'

'You can find it yourself. You can scarcely miss it. Head north and when it feels wet you've reached the sea.'

'Do Boris and Rose like the sea?'

'I... Yes.' Keep it formal. Keep it formal.

'I'll go and see it by myself, then, shall I?'

'If you like.' Keep quiet, dummy.

'It's safe for swimming?'

'It's great for swimming.'

'I'll get changed then,' he said. 'I'll be back for lunch.'

Keep quiet. Keep quiet...

She couldn't keep quiet.

'I can't get down to the beach by myself,' she said, sense disappearing and desperation taking over.

This had been the hardest part of living here with Rose. With her weak legs, the track was too steep to negotiate carrying a baby, and to live so close and not have access almost killed her. She could only go to the beach when someone was there to help carry Rose. 'Not with…' Say it, she told herself. Say it. 'I—I have a b-bad leg,' she stammered.

He paused. He looked at her.

Formality took a slight backward step.

'You can't get down to the beach?'

'Not carrying Rose.'

'But you like the beach?'

'I love the beach. So does Boris and so does Rose. We all love it.'

'So if I carried Rose…'

To hell with formality. 'We could all go,' she said, enthusiasm taking over. 'I could pack a hamper. We could take an umbrella and a rug for Rose to snooze on when she gets tired.'

'How long are we staying?' he demanded, startled.

'Hours and hours,' she said happily. 'If I'm leaving this place for good in a few days, then I need all the sea I can get. When this place is a luxury hotel it'll be beyond my reach for the rest of my life.'

'So all I have to do is carry Rose.'

'And the hamper. And the picnic basket and rug. You may have to take two trips.'

'You're a manipulator.'

'The beach is worth it.'

CHAPTER FOUR

HE CARRIED the hamper, the beach umbrella and the rug down to the beach and left them there. Boris accompanied him, bounding down the track with the air of a dog about to meet canine heaven. When Hamish returned for the next load, Boris bounded up again, panting with expectancy, seeming as anxious as Susie was that his pseudo-mistress wasn't left behind. Susie was waiting, dressed in a pale lemon sarong, her arms full of Rose and Rose's necessities.

'Hamish will take us to the sea,' Susie told Rose, handing her over, and the little girl beamed, leaned over and wrapped her arms around Hamish's neck.

He froze. The feel of a baby's arms felt…weird. Really weird.

Hamish had never held a baby in his life and he'd expected it—her—to cry or at least hold herself rigid. Instead of which she clung happily to his neck and started crooning, 'Ee, ee, ee…'

'She hasn't quite got the hang of S,' Susie told

him, and Rose giggled as if her mother had just made a wonderful joke.

'You're OK to get down yourself?' he asked, and Susie's smile turned to a glower in an instant.

'I've got down under worse conditions than this. Some I'll tell you about it. You take Rose and I'll follow.'

So he did, but he carried Rose slowly, not wanting to get too far ahead of Rose's mother, aware that the climb was a struggle for Susie and she hurt more than she admitted. He thought suddenly that what he really wanted to do was scoop her up in his arms and carry her down, but even if he hadn't been carrying her child he knew that she'd swipe away any such effort.

But finally they reached the sand. Boris was off chasing seagulls. The little cove was deserted. Susie lifted Rose from his arms and started undressing her—and Hamish had time to look around him and take stock.

He'd never seen a beach like this. It was a cove, sheltered from rough seas or winds by two rocky outcrops reaching three or four hundred yards from either side of the beach. The little cove was maybe two or three hundred yards long—no more. The sand was soft, golden and sun-warmed. There were two vast eucalypts somehow emerging from the base of the cliffs to throw dappled shade if you wanted to be in the shade. There were rock pools toward the end of the cove. The waves at one end of the cove were high enough to form low surf, but at the more sheltered end there were no waves at all. Here the water sloped out gently, making the sea a nursery pool to beat the finest nursery pool anyone could ever imagine.

'You see why I cracked and asked for help?' Susie asked. She was kneeling on the rug, removing Rosie's nappy and plastering her with sunblock. 'I can't bear not to be down here.'

'Why did you have to crack before you asked?'

She hesitated. 'I don't like to ask for help.'

'It's more than that, isn't it?' he said. 'You're afraid of me?'

'No. I…'

'What did my cousin do to you?'

'It's not that.'

'Tell me.'

She flinched. Carefully she replaced the tube of sunblock in her holdall and then set her naked daughter on the sand. Rose started crawling determinedly toward Boris. Seeing Boris was chasing gulls in circles, here was an occupation that was going to take some time.

Hamish waited, giving Susie space. Finally she sat back on her heels and gazed out to sea.

'They were both your cousins,' she whispered. 'Kenneth and Rory. Kenneth killed Rory so he'd inherit all this—and when he discovered I was pregnant he tried to kill me as well. He hauled me and my twin, Kirsty, onto a boat right here in this cove and tried to drive us onto rocks.' She shivered but then gave a tentative smile. 'But we're tough. No one messes with the McMahon twins.'

'You're a twin?'

'Yep. And proud of it. Kirsty fell for the local doctor and they married last year. She now has two little stepdaughters and is fast becoming a local.'

'But you want to go home?'

'My life is in the States. It's time to get on with it. You either get on with life or you die,' she said simply. 'I was a mess for a while, but I've come out the other side.'

'So why are you afraid of me?'

'I'm not afraid.'

'I think you are.'

'Rose needs a swim,' she said, almost angrily. 'It's too good a day to mess with by talking about what's past.'

'I agree,' he told her. 'I could use a swim, too.'

'The wave end is better for swimming,' she told him. 'Rose and I use the end without waves.'

'Different ends. Now, how did I know you were going to say that?'

'Just swim,' she snapped. 'Enough with the psychoanalysis. This might be the last time I swim in this place and I intend to enjoy it.'

Susie spent the next hour in the shallows and she was aware of Hamish every single minute. She took Rosie up to her knees in water, then sat with the little girl on her lap while the wavelets washed over them. Rosie splashed and cooed and giggled and Susie giggled with her—but still she watched Hamish.

He was a strong swimmer, she decided. He used a clean, efficient stroke that said he'd been properly trained and he wasn't out of practice. He took no chances in an unknown environment, not going deeper than chest depth but stroking strongly from one end of the cove to the other and back again. When he wearied of swimming he bodysurfed, catching the white breakers with an ease that said he'd done this, too.

He was glorying in the water, in the sun and in the day just as much as she was, she thought. She watched his lithe body slicing through the water with something akin to jealousy. He looked free. He was free to live in this place if he wanted.

He didn't want. He intended to make money from it and leave.

Finally Rose started wearying. She curled into her mother's lap and snuggled and Susie struggled upright and carried her daughter up the beach to dry her off and give her lunch. She fed Rose and gave her a bottle.

While she fed her daughter Hamish still didn't come near. Instead he threw driftwood over and over into the waves for Boris. Boris would take as much of this as anyone would give him, and Hamish gave him a lot, but as Rose snuggled down and closed her eyes in satisfied sleep, Hamish came jogging up the beach to join them.

He looked fantastic, Susie thought. Wide shoulders tapering to narrow hips, not an ounce of spare flesh on him, his tanned skin coated in a fine mist of sand, his black curls flopping forward making him look almost endearing…

Cut it out! she told herself urgently. Get your hormones back where they belong.

'There are sandwiches here,' she managed. 'Rose and I have eaten. Would you like some?'

'Food!' He fell to his knees like a man who hadn't seen food for a week and as he bit into her sandwiches Susie had another of those…moments. Watching him enjoy the food she'd prepared…

There was nothing sexy about it at all, she told herself crossly, but she knew that she lied.

'You swim well,' she told him, and if she sounded stiff and formal there wasn't a blind thing she could do about it.

'I was raised in California,' he told her. 'I'm an original beach bum. I've never seen a beach as good as this, though.'

'You're still tanned.'

'I have a penthouse with a sunroof. And a heated pool.'

Oh, of course.

'You're just a paddler?' he asked, polite as well.

She thought, Drat him. How dared he put her in this state of she didn't know what?

'I like swimming.'

'You weren't swimming,' he pointed out, and she flushed.

'Right, like I can swim when I have an attached fourteen-month-old.'

'You'd like to swim?' he asked, and she bit back another angry retort.

'I'm fine.'

'Rose is asleep. You could swim now.'

'I don't like leaving Rose on the beach by herself.'

'She's not by herself,' he said gently. 'She's with me.'

So she was. Her baby was soundly asleep. She wouldn't wake for a couple of hours. Hamish was offering her freedom, and she'd really, really like a swim.

But something was holding her back. Not distrust, exactly. More...

She couldn't put a finger on it.

'You can trust me,' he said, forcing her to try.

'I know.'

'You'll be able to see her all the time you're swimming. Go on, Susie, you know you'd love to.'

She would.

'What's stopping you?'

'Nothing.'

'Swim,' he told her. 'Or I'll lift you up and hurl you into the waves with my bare hands.'

'I'd like to see you try.'

'I wouldn't,' he confessed. 'I might have inherited a title, but Big Bad Sir Brian Blipping Villagers On the Head is a far cry from a wimpish stockbroker who values his back.'

It was only Hamish who was making her nervous. Swimming didn't.

Susie did this often, whenever Kirsty brought her twins over. They'd take turns to play childminder while the other took off into deep water and gloried in the freedom the water allowed.

It did allow freedom. The car accident that had killed Rory had damaged Susie's spine. Slowly, slowly she was recovering from the damage it had caused but she wasn't free to walk and run as she'd like. Stiffness and residual pain held her back.

But in the water...

She'd always been better than Kirsty in the water. She'd captained her junior-high waterpolo team. She'd been selected to play for the state, and only the fact that her life had got busy had stopped her going further. But for Susie swimming was an extension of breathing.

Now she walked stiffly into the water, stood for one lovely, lingering, anticipatory moment—and then knifed forward into an oncoming wave.

Gorgeous. Just gorgeous. The moment she was through the breaker she felt her other life kick in, the life she'd known before the accident, before Rory's death, before motherhood. She was a girl again, free, her body whole and healthy and ready for whatever the day should bring.

It almost gave her the courage to face the future.

She turned to the beach and Hamish was watching. Even from here she could see that he was tense. He was sitting on the sand with Boris beside him. His arm was draped over the dog. Rosie was curled up close by, sound asleep in the shade, but Hamish was still in the sun. He should be lying on the sun-warmed sand and snoozing, she thought, but he was bolt upright, watching.

He was playing lifeguard, she thought suddenly, recognising his tension for what it was. If she got into trouble he'd be down here in a minute, surging to her rescue.

She waved. He waved back but the tension didn't ease.

She grinned—and then the smile died.

She liked it, she realised. She liked it a lot that he was playing lifeguard for her.

Who'd play lifeguard for her when she went back to the States?

You won't need a lifeguard, she told herself fiercely. You'll be fine. Don't even think that you might still need someone. You've been depressed before and you're not getting depressed again.

She turned to face the other end of the cove. She put her head down—and she swam.

Hamish watched as Susie limped down to the shore-line and was…astonished. She was beautiful, he thought. Gorgeous.

But she was also damaged. She was wearing a

bikini that showed off every lovely curve, but it also revealed a wide, jagged scar across the small of her back. Was this the back injury that caused her limp?

She'd lost a husband. She was raising a baby on her own.

He was kicking her out of her castle.

Something inside his gut clenched as he watched her walk into the waves. Emotional decisions were not appropriate here, he told himself fiercely. This castle was worth a small fortune—no, a large fortune—and to keep a woman and a baby here in perpetuity was ridiculous. The lawyers had told him she'd been well provided for, and she'd reiterated that herself. She could go back to America and get on with whatever life she'd had before she'd met this Rory character and been dragged into this make-believe fantasy of titles and castles and…emotion.

He continued to watch as she stood, thigh deep in the waves, seeming to simply soak in the sun. She gazed about her as if taking in the sheer beauty of the cove, though she must have seen it so many times.

She stilled, then knifed forward into the oncoming wave and he forgot about the beauty of the cove.

She simply disappeared. Her dive into the wave produced nary a splash. Her body became a streamlined torpedo, slicing down and under, and it was as if she'd never been there.

She didn't surface.

He was standing up, startling Boris who'd had his ears resting on his knees. Boris barked, expecting adventure, but Hamish had his eyes shaded. He was moving forward, trying to see…

She surfaced finally fifty yards from where she'd gone under. One breath, a slight turn and then down under again, and he was searching once more.

Where…where…?

Twenty yards this time, only twenty yards and she was moving along the cove rather than out to sea. Another breath, hardly perceptible—the break of her head above water could hardly be seen—and then under again, swift and sure, like a sleek young seal, surfacing to breathe but all economy of effort underwater.

He'd never seen anything like it. He thought he was a good swimmer, but she was magnificent.

He'd run a few steps in those first panicked seconds and Boris was bouncing around his legs, barking, expecting excitement. He lifted a piece of driftwood and threw it into the shallows, pretending to any unseen onlooker that he'd stood specifically to do this. That he hadn't panicked. That the sight of Susie moving with such economy of action—with such beauty—didn't have the power to move him.

Only, of course, it did have the power to move him. He felt…

He didn't know how he felt.

Boris came streaming back up the beach, hauling his driftwood for another throw. The stick was laid at his feet and the big dog shook, sending a spray of sand and sea, hauling Hamish's thoughts back to reality. To at least some semblance of normality.

'I'm going back to babysitting,' he told Boris. 'I'm not watching.'

Boris put his head on the side and gazed at him in mute enquiry.

'Well, I'm hardly a lifesaver,' he muttered, sitting on the beach, hugging the dog and staring out to sea. 'She can swim better than I can. There's nothing I can do for your mistress, boy, except sit with her sleeping baby and give her a few more moments' freedom.'

She waved from behind the breakers and he waved back.

Freedom…

She was glorying in her freedom, he thought, and suddenly he remembered his office back in Manhattan. It was a magnificent office. He had plate-glass windows that looked all the way to the Statue of Liberty in New York Harbor.

There was still plate glass between him and the sea.

'It's just because you've never had a holiday that

you're thinking like this,' he told himself, suddenly angry. 'Get over it. Cut it out with the emotion, Douglas. You know where that gets you, and you don't want to go there.'

He lay back on the sand and closed his eyes.

Then he half opened one. Then he shrugged and sat up.

He'd just watch.

It had been a fabulous swim.

Susie came out of the water laughing with delight, pleasure and sheer wellbeing. OK, she was leaving this place, but its memories would stay with her for ever and one of them was this day. She shook herself like Boris, holding her hands out and wiggling her whole body so a spray of water went everywhere. Boris, who'd bounded down the beach to meet her, backed off as the water hit him, and she laughed with delight at her neat reversal of roles.

She looked up the beach and Hamish was watching her. She switched back. She'd had her time out.

Back to being the castle relic.

She walked up the beach and he rose to meet her, holding out her towel. She hesitated for a moment, just because the gesture seemed curiously intimate.

Which was dumb. It meant nothing. How many

times had Kirsty done the same thing? She took the towel and retired behind it, enveloping her whole face so she didn't have to look at him.

'Best beach in the world,' he said softly, and she let her towel drop to her shoulders and tried to smile.

'It is.'

'You'll hate leaving it.'

'I will. But I've had it for over a year. It's time for someone else to enjoy it.' Her smile became a little more determined. 'Or many someones. All the people who'll come to your hotel.'

'It's the sensible thing to do, to sell it.'

'It is.'

'You will be all right?'

'I'll be fine,' she told him, determined. 'Thank you for looking after Rose.'

'I've never babysat before.'

'Never?'

'No.'

'No family?'

'No brothers or sisters. An older cousin who was a creep.'

'I think that'd be awful,' she said. 'Being an only kid. Being a twin was wonderful.'

He thought about that, and looked down at her sleeping baby. Another only kid? 'Rose…'

'I'll surround her with kids,' she said, deter-

mined. How was she going to do that? She didn't
have a clue.

She was going home to juggle baby, career, life.

She was not going to let it get her down.

'Your sister's here?'

'Yes.'

'She has kids.'

'Yes.'

'Why don't you stay here?'

'And be dependent on Kirsty for the rest of my
life? No, thanks very much.'

'Independence can be hard.'

'I suspect you're a master of it,' she said. 'I'm just
learning but I'll manage.'

'Susie…' he began—and then paused as the
sound of a motor cut the stillness. He turned to
watch a dinghy putt-putt around the cove. It was a
simple, two-person craft with a small motor that
would have been dangerous on a day that was any
less calm than this. But it was calm and the two
people in the boat looked inordinately pleased with
themselves. A middle-aged couple—the man in a
loud Hawaiian shirt and the woman in a swimsuit
that had even more gardenias on than her husband's
shirt—were heading straight for them.

As they came within earshot the man stood up in
the boat, rocked precariously and yelled.

'Ahoy. Can we land on this beach? Are there rocks?'

'No rocks,' Susie yelled back, relieved her tete-a-tete was over.

They cruised towards the shore, a bit too fast. Neither got out of the boat until it hit sand. Then they sat in the rocking boat, removed their sandals with care and put their toes into the water as if expecting piranhas.

No piranhas.

'Ooh, it's lovely, Albert,' the lady said. 'It's not too cold at all.' She turned to them and beamed a welcome. 'Hi.'

They were Americans. The place was starting to be overrun with Americans, Susie thought. 'Hi,' she replied, while Hamish said nothing at all.

'We just wanted to take your picture,' the woman told her, beaming still. 'That's right, isn't it, Albert? We brought the boat round from Dolphin Bay harbour and I saw you through the fieldglasses with your baby asleep and your puppy, and you all look beautiful. I bet that dog's got dingo in him, I said. And I said to Albert, I'd like to take their picture, because you remind me so much of what we were at that age. And now life's an adventure and it's wonderful but I just thought…seeing you two…' Her beam faded a little. 'You don't mind, do you?' she asked, suddenly anxious that she might have offended the natives. 'If you give me your name and address I'll send you a copy. Albert is a lovely photographer.'

Albert looked bashful, but combined beam and bashful very nicely.

'We're only in Australia for a week,' the woman went on. 'For five of those days Albert has a conference but I said I wasn't going home before I'd met some real Australians. So I got a pin and closed my eyes and stuck it in a map of places we could get to from Sydney and here we are. And I know you aren't aboriginal or anything, but you so look like you belong. Anyway, can we take your picture?'

'Um,' Susie said with a sideways glance at the silent Hamish. 'What do you think...luv?'

He grinned. Her drawl had been an attempt to sound Australian but she hadn't quite managed it.

'Geez, darl, I dunno why not,' he drawled, and his accent was so much better than hers that she almost laughed out loud. 'We could do with one of them photo thingies to show the kiddies when they grow up.'

She choked. Albert suddenly looked suspicious.

'They might already have a camera, Honey.'

'We'd be very pleased to have our picture taken,' Susie said. This was such a glorious morning, she was determined that everyone could enjoy it. She glared at Hamish. 'What my…what he meant was that'd it'd be an honour to have a picture taken by an American.'

'That's all right, then,' Honey said, obviously thinking the same thing. 'Can you cuddle? I don't suppose you want to pick the baby up?'

'She's just gone to sleep,' Susie said. Enough was enough. But then she grinned and leaned down, hoisted the wet and sand-coated dog up and thrust him into Hamish's arms. 'There you go, darl,' she said. 'You cuddle the dingo.'

The dingo stuck his nose into Hamish's face and slurped.

'Gee,' Hamish managed. 'Thanks…darl.'

'Just stand behind the baby,' Honey urged. 'So we can get you all in the shot.'

They did, bemused.

'Put your arm round her,' Albert urged.

'It's all I can do to hold the dingo,' Hamish muttered. Boris was wiggling like the crazy mutt he was. Ecstatic.

'I'll hold the back half,' Susie said and did that, catching Boris's legs.

The dog was now upside down, his front end held by Hamish and his back half held by Susie.

'Now cuddle your wife,' Albert said,

'She's not—'

'Cuddle me, darl,' Susie said sweetly. 'You know you want to.'

He cuddled her. He stood on the sun-warmed beach, with a dog in his arms, with Rose curled up asleep at his feet, with a woman pressed against him and with his arm around her, and he smiled at the camera as if he meant it.

It was like an out-of-body experience, he thought. If Marcia could see him now she'd think he must have an identical twin. This was nothing like he was. The self-contained Hamish Douglas was a world away. He should be in his office now, with his hair slicked down, wearing a suit and tie, in charge of his world.

Instead…

Susie was leaning against him. She was still cool to the touch after her swim. He'd been getting hot on the beach and the cool of her body against his was great.

Not just the cool. The smell of her. The feel of her…

She curved right where she ought to curve. His arm held her close and she used her free arm to tug him even closer. The feel of her fingers on his hip, the strength of her tugging him close….

Whew.

He smiled at the camera but it was all he could do to manage it.

He needed to go home, he thought. He needed to put this place on the market and get out of here.

Why was he terrified?

A vision of his mother came back, his mother late at night, coming into his room, putting her head on his bed and sobbing her heart out.

'I never should have loved. If I'd known it'd hurt like this, I never, never would have loved him. Oh, God, Hamish, the pain…'

He withdrew. His arm dropped and Susie felt it and moved aside in an instant. It had been play-acting, he knew. She hadn't meant to hold him, to curve against him as if she belonged.

'Where shall we send the pictures?' Honey asked, aware as they moved apart that the photo session was definitely over. There was something in their body language that told her there was no way she'd get them back together again. 'Do you have a permanent address? Somewhere we can send a letter?'

Susie gazed at her blankly.

'These people think we're dole bludgers, sleeping in the back of a clapped-out ute,' Hamish said, and managed a grin at his mastery of the language. And the knowledge that went with it. Ute—short for utility vehicle—a pick-up truck. And dole bludger?

He'd heard the term on the plane. They'd been flying over the coast and the man in the seat beside him had waved to the beach below.

'There's a major social security problem in Australia,' he'd told Hamish. 'The weather's so good and the surf's so good there's an army of kids who refuse to work. They go on social security—the dole—and spend their life surfing. Go up and down the coast looking for good surf, sleeping in the back of utes. Bloody dole bludgers'll be the ruination of this country.'

And it was too much for Susie. He saw the mischief lurking in her eyes and the laughter threatening to explode, and he opened his mouth to stop her but it was too late.

'We're no dole bludgers,' she told them, in a tone of offended virtue. 'And in truth we're not husband and wife. I'll have you know that this…' she pointed to Hamish as she'd point to some mummified Egyptian remains '…is Lord Hamish Douglas, Earl of Loganaich. His address, of course, is Loganaich Castle, Dolphin Bay. And me… I'm the castle relic. And gardener and dogsbody besides.' She motioned to Rose at her feet. 'There's always a baby in these sorts of situations,' she told them. 'But it's probably wiser not to ask any more questions.'

* * *

'You realise they'll still think we're dole bludgers,' Hamish said, when he could get a grip on his laughter and was attempting to get a grip on reality. The couple were putt-putting back out of the cove, with Albert pausing to take one more shot before they rounded the headland and disappeared from view.

'Yeah, we're high on dope. I'll probably get a visit from Social Security.' Susie chuckled. 'I should have told them I was an Arabian princess. We would have just as much chance at belief.'

'But we've made their morning,' Hamish said. The tension he felt as he'd held Susie was dissipating, changing to something different. Shared pleasure in the pure ridiculousness of the moment. Laughter. It was a laughter he hadn't felt before. He felt…free. 'They've got more local colour than they bargained for.'

'What's the bet they go into the post office when they go back?'

'The post office?'

'Harriet's the postmistress and she has a huge sign out the front advertising information. Collecting and imparting information is a passion. If they go in and say they've met a crazy beach bum who calls himself a lord, they'll get told exactly what's what and they'll be back here for more pictures.'

'We'll retire behind our castle walls and pull up the drawbridge.'

'If only it were that easy,' Susie said, and the laughter slipped a little. 'I… Maybe we should go up now. I want to get some paving done this afternoon.'

'I need to do some cataloguing.'

'Cataloguing?'

'Marcia says I should make lists of contents.'

'Sure.' She eyed him with more than a little disquiet. 'What will you do with Ernst and Eric?'

'Who?'

'Suits of armour.'

'Um…' He'd seen them. Of course he'd seen them. One could hardly miss them. 'I might give them to a welfare shop,' he ventured. 'If I can find a welfare shop that'll take them.'

'I'll buy them.'

'Why on earth,' he said cautiously, 'would you want two imitation suits of armour that stand eight feet high and are enough to scare the socks off anyone who comes near?'

'When I go home I won't have Boris,' she said with dignity. 'I need Eric and Ernst. Besides, they're excellent conversationalists. We've reached consensus on most important political points but the ramifications of the Kyoto agreement in developing countries still needs some fine tuning.'

He stared at her.

Then he burst out laughing.

She looked affronted. 'You can't think the ramifications of such an agreement are a laughing matter?'

'No,' he said at once, wiping the grin off his face. 'They're very serious indeed. Only last week I was telling my potted palm—'

'There's no need to mock.'

'I'm not mocking. But Ernst and Eric are yours,' he told her. 'Absolutely. Who am I to separate a woman from her political sparring partners? How are you going to get them home?'

'I guess they won't let me take them on the plane?'

'You could see if you could get them diplomatic passports. I could make a few phone calls. Eric and Ernst, born in China and holding views that are decidedly left-wing...or I assume they're left-wing?'

'It's dangerous to assume anything about Ernst and Eric,' she said in a voice that was none too steady.

'I won't. I'll approach the situation with diplomatic caution. But we'll do our best, Susie Douglas. When you leave for America I'd very much like to see Ernst on one side of you on the plane and Eric on the other.'

'Eric is a vegetarian,' she said with such promptness that he blinked. 'And Ernst hates sitting over a wing.'

He choked. She was standing in front of him, all

earnestness, the sun glinting on her gorgeous hair, the laughter in her eyes conflicting with the prim schoolteacher voice and he felt…he felt…

'I'll see what I can do,' he managed. 'But meanwhile I think we should pack up for the day. I think I've had a bit too much sun.'

CHAPTER FIVE

THEY were formal for the rest of the day. Formal to the point of avoiding each other. Hamish did a bit of cataloguing but there wasn't much point cataloguing imitation chandeliers. Susie did a bit of packing but her heart wasn't in that either.

They met briefly for dinner. 'Soup and toast,' Susie decreed, and Hamish didn't argue. He ate his soup and toast, and then later, when Susie had gone to bed, he ate more toast. Tomorrow he'd have to go on a forage into town and find some decent food, he decided. Then he remembered the next day was the day of the fête and he felt so faint-hearted that he stopped feeling hungry and went back to bed and stared at the ceiling for a while.

He was right out of his comfort zone. Jodie had told him this was a holiday. Weren't holidays meant to make you feel rested?

The sounds of the sea were wafting in his open window but the rest of the world was silent. After the buzzing background hum of Manhattan this seemed like another world. It was so silent it sounded…noisy? The absence of traffic sounds was like white noise.

He lay and listened and decided he was homesick for Manhattan. For his black and grey penthouse, his austere bathroom without kings or queens watching from gilt frames, for his traffic noise…

For Marcia? Of course for Marcia.

Who was he kidding? He wasn't homesick. He didn't know what he was. Finally he drifted into sleep where Marcia and Jodie and Susie all jostled for position. Marcia was silently, scornfully watching. Jodie was standing with hands on hips, daring him to be different. Susie was laughing.

But while he watched, Susie's laughter turned to tears and he woke in a cold sweat.

And Susie was no longer in his dream. She was standing in the open doorway and she was neither laughing or crying.

She was holding a kilt.

'Behold your valet, my lord,' she told him. 'Your kilt and all your other various appendages await your noble personage.'

He sat up fast. Then he remembered he wasn't wearing pyjamas. He grabbed his sheet—and he blinked at the apparition in the doorway.

Susie was dressed in tartan.

She wasn't wearing a kilt. She was wearing royal blue Capri pants, stretching neatly around every delicious curve, and a gorgeous little top, in the same tartan as the kilt she was holding out for him to wear. Her hair was tied up in some complex knot on top, and it was caught up in a tartan ribbon.

'What are you staring at?' she asked.

'The tartan…'

'You might be the head of the clan but I'm a Douglas, too.'

This woman was his family, he thought, dazed.

Move on. Family was a scary thought. His eyes fell to the kilt she was holding out.

'I'm not wearing that.'

'You promised,' she said with something akin to forcefulness. 'You can't back out now, your Lordship. I've promised as well.'

'You've promised?'

'Well, you promised first. You said you would, and now I've telephoned the organisers and they've told everyone you're coming. They've trucked in the Barram pipe band with an extra piper this year, 'cos last time the piper had a wee bit too much whisky on the bus on the way here and didn't perform to expectation. So there's two pipers to pipe you on stage, your

Lordship, and a whole pipe band besides, and the Brownies are doing a guard of honour especially.'

'The Brownies?' To say he was hornswoggled was an understatement. 'What on earth are Brownies?'

'Scary little brown persons,' she said. 'You must have heard of them. They sell cookies and do bob-a-job, only now it's two dollars and you have to sign forms in triplicate saying they can't hurt themselves when they shine your shoes.'

'I'm lost,' he complained, and she grinned.

'Fine. Stay that way. Ask no questions, just smile and wave like the Queen Mum. You want me to help you to dress?'

'No!'

'Only offering. I thought you might have trouble with your sporran.'

'An earl,' he said with cautious dignity, 'especially the ninth Earl of Loganaich of the mighty clan Douglas, can surely manage his own sporran.'

'Tricky things, sporrans.'

'Not to us earls.'

'Well, then,' she said cheerfully. She walked across and dumped a kilt, what looked like a small mountain of spare tartan fabric, tassles and toggles, a purse of some description and a beret with a feather on his bedside chair. Boris followed behind, looking interested.

'There you go, your Lordship,' she said happily. 'Everything you need to look shipshape. Come on, Boris.'

'Boris can help,' he said graciously, and her grin widened.

'I'll leave you with your valet, then, shall I, my lord? Porridge in the kitchen in thirty minutes?'

'Toast.'

'If you're wearing a sporran you need porridge.'

'Toast,' he said in something akin to desperation. 'As the leader of your clan I demand toast.'

She chuckled. 'Ooh, I love a forceful man…in a kilt.'

'Susie…'

She got her features back under control with difficulty. She was back to a grin only. 'Your wish is my command,' she said. 'Sir.' He got a sharp salute, clicked heels and she was gone, leaving him alone with his valet.

'Boris…' he said cautiously, eyeing his pile of tartan as if it might bite. 'What do you think a sporran might be?'

It took him a while. It took him close to an hour, really, but if he was going to do this thing he might as well do it right. By the time he had every pleat in place, every toggle where it was supposed to be toggling, and the feather in his cap at just the right angle he felt like he'd done a full day's work. He gazed in the mirror and thought he had done a good day's work. He looked unbelievable.

Boris was sitting watching with the patience of all good valets, and when Hamish finally adjusted his cap and looked at the final result the dog gave a deep low woof, as if in appreciation.

'Not bad at all,' Hamish told the dog. 'I wish Jodie could see me now.'

And Marcia?

Marcia couldn't help but be impressed with this, he thought, but it was Jodie he thought of. Jodie would look at him and whistle, and giggle.

Like Susie giggled. Susie and Jodie…

Two unlikely women in his life. Jodie was no longer part of what he did. She was making choir stalls with her Nick. Ridiculous. How could she make any money doing that?

And Susie… In a couple of weeks Susie would be a memory as well and he'd be left with Marcia.

Which was the way he wanted it.

'Porridge!' The yell from below stairs startled him out of his reverie. 'On the table. Now.'

He crossed to the landing. Took a deep breath. Swelled his chest.

'Toast!' he yelled back. 'Woman!'

She emerged from the kitchen and gazed upward.

And froze. Her eyes took in his appearance, from the tip of his shoes, his long socks with their tassles, up to the feather…

He felt like blushing.

'Wow,' she said at last on a long note of awed discovery. 'Oh, Hamish, wow. They're going to love you.'

'Who?'

'All the ladies of Dolphin Bay,' she said simply. 'Me, too. What a hunk. Do you have everything in the right place?'

'I think so,' he said, still trying not to blush.

'And you've got the appropriate attire underneath?'

'Don't even go there.' He stepped back from the balustrade—fast—and she chuckled.

'No matter. I've never seen such an impressive Scottish hero—and I've seen *Braveheart*.'

'I'd imagine that those guys might be a bit handier with their weaponry than I am,' he said, still cautious. 'I'm all froth and no substance.'

'You certainly look like substance. Porridge now, sir. Double helping if you like.'

'Susie…'

'Yes, sir?'

'I thought I made myself clear. Toast.'

'There's a bit of a problem,' she confessed. 'If I'd seen your knees before this, I might have concentrated a bit more. Very good at focussing the mind, those knees.'

This was ridiculous. He wanted his kilt lowered.

'So what's happened to my toast?' he managed.

'I burnt two lots,' she confessed. 'I was thinking about Angus. And Priscilla.'

'Priscilla?'

'Angus's pumpkin. She's going to win today. Biggest pumpkin on show. I ended up with only one slice of bread left and Rose wanted that for toast fingers in her egg.' She took a deep breath and fixed him with a look that told him he was going to get a lecture, right now.

'Hamish, you might tell me you belong in New York—you might tell me you're not really an earl— but anyone seeing those knees knows for sure that you've found your home right here. You're the ninth Earl of Loganaich and you just need to forget all those silly ideas of being anyone else, including a toast eater, and learn to like porridge. Now, enough argument. I have a team of men arriving in ten minutes to help load Priscilla onto the trailer. So— what do they say? Save your breath to cool your porridge—my lord.' She smiled sweetly up at him. 'Come and get it while it's hot.'

It was like an out-of-body experience.

Firstly there was the fairground itself. It was

nestled between two hills, with the harbour and the town on one side and bushland on the other. One could stroll around the fairground, walk a short distance to the shops or to the boats, retreat into the bush—as a few young couples showed every sign of doing even this early on—or if it all got too hot one could disappear to the beach for a quick swim.

Susie pulled her little car into the parking lot and Hamish gazed around, stunned. It was a fantastic, colourful mix of everything. Everyone. Grizzled farmers, kids with fairy floss, old ladies in wheelchairs. Gorgeous young things kitted to the nines in full dressage gear ready for the equestrian events. Kids in bathing costumes, obviously torn between beach and fair. A clown on stilts lurching from car to car and using the bonnets of the cars to steady himself.

The clown ended up right by them as they parked, and he lurched a little more, made a rush and hit their trailer. By the time they emerged he was dusting himself and staggering to his feet, pushing himself up against their pumpkin. Priscilla was almost as high as he was.

'You hurt that pumpkin and you're dead meat, Jake Cameron,' Susie told him, clearly unmoved by clowns tumbling into her trailer. 'If there's so much as a blemish on my pumpkin, it's disqualified.'

'Hi, Susie,' the clown said, removing a bulbous nose. 'Great to see you, too.'

'I didn't know you rode stilts.'

'I don't,' Jake said morosely. 'But the kids' schoolteacher asked for volunteers and the twins volunteered me. It's not going to work. The kids have been coaching me for weeks and all that's going to happen is that I break my neck. Who's going to fix me up then, I want to know?'

'Kirsty's really good at broken spines,' Susie said, and grinned. 'Or failing that, she's specially trained in palliative care. If you die you'll die in the best of hands.' She turned to Hamish, who was feeling vaguely better that he wasn't the only ridiculously clad person here. 'Hamish, this is Dr Jake Cameron. Jake's my brother-in-law. Jake and Kirsty are Dolphin Bay's doctors.'

'Hey!' Jake said, holding out a red-gloved, vast-fingered paw. 'You're the new earl. Welcome to Dolphin Bay, mate. You want to find a beer?'

Beer sounded fantastic to Hamish—but Susie's hand was on his arm and she was holding on like he wasn't going anywhere.

'Hamish is due at the opening ceremony in ten minutes.'

'No beer until you've done your duty,' Jake said sympathetically. 'But me… I've been all round the fairground on these damned stilts, risking life and limb at every step. I've added local colour for all I'm worth and I'm done. Off duty. Beer it is.'

'So who looks after the kids when they fall off the Ferris wheel?' Susie demanded.

'Heaven forbid,' Jake said. 'But Kirsty's official medical officer for the day. She's taken the pledge for the next few months so I'm a free man.'

'Jake…' Susie said, and stopped. There was a pause. A pregnant pause. 'She's taken the pledge… Are you saying what I think you're saying?'

Jake replaced his nose. Fast. 'Whoops,' he said, backing off. 'No, I didn't say that. Gotta go. Take care of your earl.'

'I will,' Susie said, but still looking very oddly indeed at her brother-in-law. 'Where's Kirsty?'

'Avoiding you, I suspect,' Jake said. 'See you.' And he took himself off like a man hunted.

'What was that about?' Hamish asked, watching the very speedy retreat of the scarlet and purple patchwork clown.

'Oh, if she is…' Susie said. 'How can I go home?' She caught herself. 'No. I must. Business. Let's get you to the stage.'

'Do I really need to?'

'Of course you need to,' she said, astonished. 'Everyone plays their part. You're part of this community now, Hamish Douglas, like it or not, and at least we're not asking you to say your speech while you're wearing stilts.'

His speech was astonishing all by itself.

The sensation of being piped onto the stage, of every face in the fairground straining to see him, of a gasp of approval as he finally reached the dais and the sound of the pipes fell away…

Susie was right, he thought, appreciating the drama of the situation. If Angus had done this for the last forty years, this small ceremony would be sorely missed—and how much worse it would be because Angus was dead.

Times changed. The time of having a laird in Castle Douglas was over, and people had to accept it, but at least he could do as Susie suggested now. He could play his part.

Speech. He had to make a speech. Not a 'take over the company' sort of speech, not now, but something with, God help him, emotion.

Just this once.

And in the end, the words came.

'I can't replace my Uncle Angus,' he told the crowd, tentative at first but growing surer as he saw by their smiles that just standing up here in the right tartan was enough to plug the void. 'I can't replace

Lord Angus Douglas, Earl of Loganaich. I don't want to. But the house of Douglas has been associated with Dolphin Bay for so long that the connection will never die. As long as Castle Loganaich stands, we'll remember the link between castle and town. We'll remember the friendship, the love, the good times and the bad. Lord Angus's death was a low point but he lived a full life with his beloved Deirdre, both of them surrounded by this town full of their friends.' He hesitated.

'Plus the odd monarch in the bathrooms,' he added, and there was a ripple of delighted laugher. Most people here had at least heard of Queen Vic.

But Hamish hadn't yet finished. He was on a roll. Maybe he could be a lord after all. 'Angus's legacy remains in the laughter and the camaraderie I'm seeing here,' he told them. 'Angus would want— Angus would insist—that life goes on and that everyone here enjoy themselves to the full. So I, Hamish Douglas, ninth Earl of Loganaich, make this my first public decree. That this fair is officially open and that everyone here proceed to have a very good time. And after the pumpkin judging… As Lord Douglas, I decree that everyone here take home a slab of pumpkin so I don't get landed with pumpkin pie for the rest of my life.'

Hooray. He'd done it. There was cheering and

more laughter. The pipes started up again and Hamish made his way off the stage to find Susie smiling at him through tears.

'Oh, Hamish, that was wonderful.'

'There's no need to cry,' he said abruptly and turned away. Drat, he was almost teary himself.

His laughter faded. He'd almost been enjoying himself but tears always did this. They snapped him right back to dreary reality. Tears in a situation like this were ridiculous. And now, if Susie not only cried but infected him with it…

No!

'Pumpkin judging,' someone yelled. 'We're waiting on the Douglas pumpkin.'

'Ooh.' Susie's tears were gone in an instant and she turned to a middle-aged lady beside her. 'Harriet, can you take Rose for a bit?' She thrust her baby forward, but Rose obviously knew the lady who Hamish recognised as the postmistress. He'd stopped and asked directions from her when he'd arrived.

'Come on.' Susie was clutching his hand and towing him through the crowd and people were laughing and parting to let them through. 'We've got a date with destiny—right now.'

Their pumpkin won. It was the fair's biggest pumpkin, with trophy and certificate to prove it.

The second biggest was entered by a withered old man who didn't seem the least bit upset about losing.

Or maybe he did. He laughed and cheered with the rest of them when the pumpkins were weighed, but as the trophy was given to a flushed and triumphant Susie, the elderly man turned to Hamish and an errant tear was rolling down his wrinkled cheek.

More tears!

'He knew, dammit,' the old man said, and he reached out and wrung Hamish's hand so hard that it hurt. 'Your uncle was the best mate a man could have. He knew he'd beaten me this year, damn him. He knew he was a winner. I wouldn't have wanted him to go any other way but hell, I miss him.' He sniffed and his wife darted forward and hugged him and led him off to the beer tent.

Susie came down from the dais, clutching her trophy and certificate, and she watched him go and sniffed again.

'I need a hanky,' she said, helpless with her hands full, and Hamish was forced to find his—from his sporran—and then hold her trophy while she blew her nose. Hard.

'I don't want it back,' he said faintly, and she managed a smile through tears.

'I'm sorry. I know guys hate tears. It's only

Ben...' She motioned to where the old man was disappearing beerwards.

'He was crying, too,' Hamish said, and if he sounded a bit desperate then he couldn't help it.

'Aunty Susie! Aunty Susie!' There were shrieks from behind them and he turned to see two pigtailed urchins bearing down on them. Two little girls aged about five, each liberally spattered with what looked like a mix of fairy floss and chocolate ice cream, raced up to them with excitement 'Aunty Susie, Mummy's got a baby for you.'

'A baby?' Susie stood stock still and the colour drained from her face. 'I knew it. I knew...'

'What's wrong?' Hamish asked before he could help himself.

'She's pregnant. I knew...'

'Hi.' Coming up behind the twins was a woman who was the mirror image of Susie. The likeness was so extraordinary that he blinked.

'Kirsty, I presume,' he said, because Susie had retired behind his handkerchief again. Oh, for heaven's sake.

'I'm Kirsty.' A cool, firm hand was placed in his. She smiled and her smile was the same as Susie's. Or maybe not. Maybe not quite as lovely?

That was a dumb thing to think. At least this woman wasn't crying.

'Why is Susie crying?' she asked, and he looked exasperated.

'Because her pumpkin won. I think.'

He expected sympathy and mutual confusion. Instead, Kirsty dropped his hand and enveloped Susie in a hug.

'Oh, sweetheart, I'm sorry. He couldn't see...'

'He did see,' Susie said, hiccuping on a sob. 'He knew. I told you. I snuck into Ben's back yard before he died and I measured it and Angus knew his would be the winner. And I bet he can see us now.'

'Then what—?'

'The twins. They said...a baby.'

Kirsty let her arms drop. She looked exasperated. 'They didn't say a baby.'

'They did.'

'They meant a puppy.'

'A puppy?' Susie lowered the handkerchief and looked out cautiously from behind it. Ready to retire again at any minute. 'What do you mean?'

'This.' Kirsty motioned behind her. 'We want our Boris back, but we've decided you need a dog.'

A small boy was bringing up the rear. He was carrying... What was he carrying?

A puppy.

The puppy was just about the weirdest dog Hamish had ever seen. She was brown, white and tubby, with long, floppy ears, Boris's expressive eyes, a stretched-out body with a puddingy tummy, a tail that added another twelve inches in length—and legs that were about three inches long.

'What is it?' Susie asked, cautious to say the least.

'This is our gift to you,' Kirsty said expansively and grinned. 'To stop Rose being an only child.' She motioned to the small boy holding the pup. 'Susie, this is Adam, and Adam's pup. Now she's your pup.'

'What…?'

'She's courtesy of Boris,' she explained, sounding exasperated. 'You know Jake inherited Boris from Miss Pritchard? Jake sort of assumed—as Boris was eight years old and Miss Pritchard was a civically responsible person—that Boris would have been neutered in the long distant past. OK, he should have checked, but he didn't. He didn't really think about it, until Adam's dachshund came into season. We share a back fence and events took their course. Even then we didn't realise until Daisy Dachshund produced one sad pup. Now that she's a few weeks old, the father's obvious.'

'Sad pup?' Susie said warily, while Hamish looked on, much as one might look through a time screen to another world.

'Well, maybe she's not exactly sad, are you, sweetheart?' Kirsty said, lifting the pup from

Adam's hands and holding her up for inspection. 'Maybe she's more…loopy. She's just won cutest puppy in show. Pup, meet Susie. Susie, meet pup.'

'Hi, pup,' Susie said, still cautious.

The pup wagged her tail. Her whole body wriggled, like a cute and furry eel.

'Anyway, Jake and I were watching the puppy judging and it suddenly occurred to us that if you're insisting on returning to America you need something to remember us by. And something to guard you. What better than a pup? We talked to Adam's parents and, amazingly, they're delighted. Even Adam's cool with it. I don't think this puppy fits what he thinks of as a real boy's dog. I know there'll be issues with quarantine but the dog-judging people say it's possible to take pups into the US from here, and Jake and I will pay.'

Susie seemed almost overwhelmed. She sniffed. 'Oh, Kirsty…'

'I don't have any more handkerchiefs,' Jake said, desperate.

'You need a truckload when Susie's around,' Kirsty said cheerfully. 'What do you think, Suze?'

'Oh,' Susie said, taking the puppy and holding her close. 'Oh…'

'I think I hear a beer calling,' Hamish said faintly. 'Is Jake in the beer tent?'

Kirsty grinned at him, not unsympathetic. 'We're all a bit much, aren't we? But your speech… All I had to do was look at you and I got teary.'

'Susie!' Harriet, the postmistress, was making her way determinedly through the crowd toward them, carrying Rose toward her mother. 'I think your daughter needs a nappy change.'

Hamish was backing already but he backed a few more feet at that. Fast. 'I can definitely hear a beer calling,' he muttered.

But Harriet wasn't about to let Hamish escape. 'Ooh, look at you,' she exclaimed, and thrust Rose at her mother, who proceeded to juggle toddler and puppy with aplomb. The elderly postmistress put an arm round Hamish's shoulders and beamed in possessive enthusiasm. She was a big lady, buxom and beaming, with a tight frizzed perm and painted lips that seemed to have a life of their own. 'Look at me,' she crowed. 'Me and Lord Hamish. Take a picture of us, someone, so I can put it up on the post-office wall.'

'I need—'

'Hey, but it shouldn't be me.' Harriet suddenly corrected herself, whisking herself out of his arms and thrusting Susie forward with an air of enormous personal sacrifice. 'It should be you. Oh, Susie, wouldn't that be something? You and the new laird. Two Douglases finally finding their place, side by side.'

Susie choked, but she had no say in the matter. She'd been thrust next to Hamish and cameras were flashing, just the same as they'd been yesterday on the beach, only worse.

Much worse.

Hamish Douglas was suddenly being photographed with Mrs Douglas, Rosie Douglas and dog.

Things were spiralling out of control here, Hamish thought desperately, and a man had to do what a man had to do.

He put Susie—and appendages—carefully away from him and took two more steps back. Two long steps back.

'I need to find Jake,' he said, in tones he hoped were careful and measured and nowhere as hysterical as he felt. 'And then… I think it's wise if I stop all conjecture about me and…me and Susie right now. I'm engaged to a young lady called Marcia Vinel and she's arriving here the day after tomorrow.'

CHAPTER SIX

HAMISH spent the rest of the day being inspected. From every angle. Susie had been right when she'd said his presence would take everyone's mind off their loss. He could not only hear the buzz his presence was making. He could feel it. He was whispered about, talked about, watched….

'I need to get this kilt off,' he told Jake. 'Did I ever wolf-whistle a woman for having great legs? Kill me now. I deserve it. Everyone's staring at my knees.'

'They're staring at the whole package,' Jake said. 'And you can forget any sympathy from this direction. You're not wearing size twenty purple and red shoes. My feet are killing me.'

'Did Susie tell me you were a surgeon in the city before you were married?' Hamish said curiously. 'What on earth made you move here?'

'Life,' Jake said, and Hamish looked out over the fairground and shuddered.

'Not my idea of life.'

'And your idea of life would be…'

'Control,' Hamish said forcefully. 'Knowing what I'm waking up to every morning.'

'I know what I'm waking up to every morning,' Jake said peaceably. 'Chaos. I wouldn't have it any other way.'

'Poles apart,' Hamish said morosely. Then he thought of another issue. 'And what the hell are you about, giving Susie a dog? Hasn't she got enough to cope with? She's got to make her way in America, get a career going. How's she going to handle a dog?'

'The heart expands to fit all comers,' Jake said and grinned. 'I'm a doctor, you know. That's a very medical sort of diagnosis.'

'Sure it does,' Hamish snapped. 'Susie's now been loaded with a mutt who she'll have to love whether she wants to or not.'

'Love isn't the same as provide for,' Jake said, looking at him curiously. 'It's a bit different. Sure, it means more work but to not accept it…'

'You're telling me there are any real advantages in her getting a dog?'

'Kirsty's her twin,' Jake said definitely. 'If Kirsty says she needs a dog, then she needs a dog. She's lonely as hell.'

'Dogs don't fix loneliness.'

'They do a bit,' Jake said. 'Anyway, the dog wasn't my decision, mate. Kirsty thinks it's a good idea and getting between the twins is like dividing the Red Sea. It'd take a force bigger than I have at my disposal. They're inseparable.'

'But Susie's going home.'

'There is that,' Jake said. He surveyed Hamish thoughtfully and Hamish lifted his beer and studied the dregs.

'If you look at me like that for any more than two more seconds I'm walking out of here and I'll keep walking till I reach America,' he said softly, and Jake grinned.

'Fair enough. You've copped a bit of matchmaking, then.'

'Just a bit. The whole fairground had gone into *Wouldn't it be great?* mode.'

'Well, it would be great.'

'Except I like my women self-contained, clever, cool and sassy.'

'Susie's clever and sassy.'

'Four or nothing,' he said, and drained his beer. 'I'm engaged to Marcia. She'll be here the day after tomorrow.'

Jake raised an eyebrow. Sussing him. And grinning. 'First I've heard of it. But it's no business of mine, mate,' he added, pushing himself to his size twenty feet. 'I have two hundred more balloons to disperse before I'm off duty. One more beer and I'll let the whole lot go skyward. Which might not be such a bad thing, if I didn't have three womenfolk who'd give me a hard time for the rest of my life. They'd probably make me blow up two hundred more.'

'Marcia would never give me a hard time over a balloon.'

'Lucky you,' Jake said. 'Or unlucky you. Depending on which way you want to look at it, but I sure as hell know what way I'm looking at it. I'll leave you to your very important phone call.'

'My…?'

'If Marcia's coming in two days, hadn't you better let her know?' Jake suggested. 'If you're arming the battlements it's always a good idea to let the armour know what's required.'

What was it about this place? He'd landed in some chaotic muddle of people who seemed to think they knew him because his name was Douglas. Who seemed to think they knew more about his life than he did.

Which was clearly ridiculous.

But Jake had said he needed to make a phone call—and Jake was right.

Calculation. Midday here. Eight at night there. Fine.

Marcia answered on the first ring. Still at her desk, then.

'Hi,' she said warmly. 'How's the valuation going?'

'I'm a bit distracted,' he told her. He'd emerged from the hubbub of noise within the beer tent, he'd retreated to the side of the marquee but he could still see the colourful chaos that was the fair. 'Our pumpkin just won a major prize.'

There was a moment's silence. Then... 'Well, hooray for our pumpkin. Hamish, are you feeling well?'

'Are you absolutely imperatively busy at the moment?'

'I'm always absolutely imperatively busy.'

'And if you dropped everything and came here...'

'Why would I do that?'

'The widow,' he said, and his desperation must have sounded down the wire because there was laughter.

'Oh, darling, I did wonder. You're the heir and she's the dowager. So there's a bit of matchmaking?'

'Not on our part. I mean...she doesn't want it any more than I do. But the townspeople do, and it'd make it much easier to keep everything on a business footing if you appeared.'

There was a moment's silence. He could imagine her scrolling down the screen of her electronic diary, juggling appointments. Figuring out imperatives.

'I can spare you three days,' she said at last. 'There's a financial review in Hong Kong starting next Friday I was tempted to attend. Hong Kong's almost your time zone so I could get over jet-lag with you. I have no intention of being in Hong Kong if my mind's not totally focussed. There's some heavy stuff going down. Oil futures. It could be really big.'

'So that means…'

'I'll be with you Monday your time. I'll fly out again on Thursday. Will that solve your problems?'

He stared around him. Oil futures in Hong Kong.

One of Jake's twins—Alice?—was walking toward him carrying a hot dog. She was leaving a trail of ketchup in her wake. She was beaming and holding it out to him as if it was a truly amazing gift.

Marcia here?

She had to come. He needed grounding. Fast.

'That'll be great,' he said weakly.

'I'll let you know the arrangements. Is there anything else you need now? I'm in a rush.'

'No.'

'Then 'bye.' Click.

'Marcia's coming,' he told Alice as he accepted her hot dog, and she gave him a dubious smile.

'Is Marcia nice?'

'Very nice.'

'Does she like hot dogs?'

'I guess.'

'My Aunty Susie says you have to come,' she said. 'The wood chopping's about to start and the laird always has first chop.'

'He's a bit of all right.'

The woodchopping had seemed just what Hamish had needed. His hands were still a bit sore from digging but he put that aside. The sight of logs, waiting to be chopped, meant that he could vent his spleen in a way that didn't hurt anyone (except him—pity about the blisters!), didn't involve so much alcohol that he'd regret it the next day and got him away from Susie.

The logs were propped as posts. The woodchoppers were given a truly excellent axe and told to go to it. Hamish did his first ceremonial chop, then watched the champion woodchoppers with something akin to envy. While he watched the woodchoppers, the inhabitants of Dolphin Bay were watching him, talking about him, clapping him on the back—and looking sideways at Susie.

Things were starting to get desperate. His blisters hurt—but would a real earl be deflected by a few blisters? Of course not.

As the novice events started, he stripped to the waist and proceeded to chop.

* * *

'There's something about a man in a kilt and nothing else,' Kirsty murmured, and nudged her sister. 'Ooh-er. A fine figure of a man, our new laird.'

'He's not our new laird,' Susie retorted, a trifle breathlessly. 'A new laird wouldn't sell his castle and run.'

'He hasn't sold it yet. There's many a slip…'

'Cut it out, Kirsty.'

'Susie, he's gorgeous.'

'Kirsty, he's engaged to be married.'

'So you have noticed he's gorgeous.'

'I'd have to be blind not to notice he's gorgeous.'

The logs had to be chopped into four. The way it was done was to chop a chunk out, ram a plank into the chunk, stand on the plank and lop the top off. Then lower the plank and start again with a lower chunk. Hamish was on his second level. Chunks of wood were flying everywhere—there was more enthusiasm than science in his technique. His body was glistening with sweat.

'Kilts are yummy,' Kirsty said thoughtfully. 'I wonder if Jake'd wear one.'

'I'm yummy enough without a kilt.' Jake had come up behind them, and now he put his arms round his wife and hugged. 'How do you improve on just plain irresistible?'

'I liked you better when you were four feet taller,' Susie told him, eyeing her brother-in-law with disfavour. 'And I don't know how it is but the red nose just doesn't cut it.'

'It turns Kirsty on, though,' Jake said smugly, and Kirsty answered by pulling his plastic nose back to the full length of its elastic, holding it thoughtfully for a moment and then letting it go.

'Yep, I like it better on,' she said, and turned back to her sister. 'Now, where were we?'

'Hey.' Jake clutched his nose in pain and Susie giggled. But there was a part of her…

There was a part of her that was really, really jealous of her sister and her husband, she decided. She'd met and fallen for Rory, but she'd had him for such a short time and then he'd been gone. His loss still had the power to hurt so much that she almost couldn't bear it. The sight of her sister and her husband so happy…

Her eyes turned involuntarily back to Hamish. Hamish smashing through his third the level of wood. Hamish concentrating every ounce of energy in getting the log through, pitting his strength against the wood.

She thought of how he'd been yesterday morning, digging her path with just such energy. What was driving him?

What was this Marcia like?

It wasn't her business.

'I'm going home,' she said abruptly. 'Harriet's over under the trees with Rosie and Pup. I'll go and collect them. I think it'd be better if I took Pup home now and settled her into her new home before dinner. Even if that home is temporary,' she added in an undertone but Kirsty heard and winced.

'Susie, do you mind? About the puppy?'

'I love Pup.' She hugged her sister.

'But Hamish…do you mind that he's taking over?'

'Well…' She shrugged. 'I can't not mind, but it doesn't make sense to care too much.'

'If you two got on…'

'We do get on. And no matter how much better we got on, he'd still sell the castle. It's the only sensible thing to do. Can you give him a ride home?'

'Sure,' Jake told her. 'If you really need to go.'

'I really need to go.'

He won.

Hamish stood over his four pieces of chopped logs and gasped until he got his breath back. This was fantastic. Much better than any gym workout. He was standing bare backed, clad only in his kilt and footwear, the sun burning on his skin, the wash of the sea the background roar to the applause of the crowd. His hands were a bit painful—actually, very painful—but what was a bit of pain? It felt like he'd been transformed into another place, another time. Another life.

He'd won.

He turned to where Susie had been standing, and she wasn't there.

'Where…?' he started, and Jake came toward him and wrung his hand.

'Well done, mate.'

'Ouch,' Hamish muttered, and hauled his hand back. 'Where's Susie?'

'Gone home.'

Right. Suddenly his hands were really, really painful.

This was dumb—but it didn't feel fantastic any more.

Hamish didn't come home for dinner and Susie didn't care. She didn't, she didn't, she didn't. She'd eaten far too much rubbish at the fair to worry about dinner—a piece of the inevitable toast was fine. She fed the puppy the mix Adam's mother had thoughtfully packed. She popped her to sleep in the wet room, and then as the puppy complained she carted her back to the kitchen, sat in the rocker in front of the fire and cuddled her.

'I'm calling you Taffy,' she said. 'I know I had sixty-three other suggestions but they can't tell me what to call my very own puppy.'

Taffy looked up at her in sleepy agreement, curled into her lap and proceeded to go to sleep.

Susie rocked on.

'Me and a puppy and a baby,' she whispered. 'I have a houseful.'

'Where will I go?' she whispered back. 'Where will I take my little family?'

She'd go back to the house she'd shared with Rory. Of course. That was the best thing to do. The simplest.

But the thought of going back to the house she'd shared with Rory…

'It'll be empty, Taf,' she told the puppy, popping her down onto a cushion by the fire. 'Even with you. It's a gorgeous house on the coast. It looks out over the ocean. It's really wild. Rory worked from home and it was great with the two of us there but…but I'm not sure you and Rosie are going to be good enough company.'

As if in answer to her question, Taffy said nothing at all.

Susie rocked on. She'd lit the range more for company than because she needed its warmth, but the gentle crackle and hiss of burning logs was comforting.

Not comforting enough.

'I have to go home.'

'Isn't talking to yourself the first sign of madness?'

She jumped close on a foot. When she came down to earth she was breathless—and cross.

'What do you think you're doing?'

'Coming home,' Hamish said and it was so much an echo of what she'd been thinking that she almost jumped again.

'You scared me.'

'I'm sorry.'

'It's your kitchen,' she said, but she sounded defensive. She took a grip and tried for a lighter note. 'You've had supper?'

But she was still flustered. He didn't look nearly as together as he'd looked that morning. He was still in his kilt but he'd chopped wood; he'd been drinking beer with the men; he'd joined the tug-of-war teams. He looked dishevelled and tired and frayed, like a Scottish lord coming home after a hard day at battle.

'You've got a splodge of toffee apple on your cheek,' she managed, a trifle breathlessly, and he wiped it away with the back of his hand and grinned.

'I've had a very good time.'

'Not like Manhattan, huh?'

'Not the least like Manhattan. I've never had a day like this in my life.'

'Do you want supper?'

'Are you kidding?' He was standing in the doorway looking big and tousled. His long socks were down at his ankles, his legs were bare and there were grass stains on his kilt. And his hair had hay in it. He looked…he looked…

Cut it out, she told herself desperately. Don't look!

'I've been judging the cooking,' he told her, still with that grin that had her heart doing those crazy somersaulting things she didn't understand at all. 'They made me honorary adjudicator, which means I've tasted scones, plum cakes, sponge cakes…you name it, I've tasted it. Some of it was truly excellent.'

'What makes you a judge?'

'It's the kilt,' he told her wisely. 'Anyone wearing a kilt like this has to know a lot about cooking. A lot about everything, really. That's why they have the House of Lords in England.'

'Sorry?'

'If you're a lord then you get to be an automatic Member of Parliament,' he told her. 'I read it somewhere. I haven't figured out whether it applies to me or not, but I guess inheriting earldomship must make me wise in some respects.'

'Like in judging scones.'

'That'd be it,' he told her, and all of a sudden they

were grinning at each other like fools. The atmosphere had changed and it was somehow…

Different.

She hadn't felt like this since Rory had died, she thought, and suddenly she felt breathless. Traitorish?

No. Free. It was like a great grey cloud, which had settled on top of her for the last two years, had lifted and she felt…extraordinary.

'You don't mind that Marcia's coming?' he said, and she caught herself and forced her stupid, floating mind back to earth with a snap.

'Of course I don't. This is your house.'

'I should have told you.'

'There was no need. There's plenty of room. And as I said, I can always move out.'

'I don't want you to move out…yet.'

Good. Great. She thought about it and wondered if she was being entirely sensible.

'I need to go,' she said a trifle uncertainly, rising and moving toward the door.

'To America?'

'Not tonight.' She managed a smile but the frisson of something different was still in the air and she felt strange. This was crazy. This man was engaged to someone called Marcia and she'd have nothing to do with him after she left here. But today… Today he'd made her smile and he'd made everyone here smile, too. She was under no illusions as to how sad a day it would have been for everyone if Hamish hadn't been here, but he'd bounced around the fair having fun, charming old ladies, eating too many scones and toffee apples, looking fabulous in his kilt. He'd given the locals something to talk about, something to smile over, and even when he left in a few weeks, even though he'd sell the castle, today had been a gift.

'Thank you,' she said simply.

'Thank you?'

'For today. Everyone loved having a laird for the day.'

'It was my pleasure.'

'Really?'

'It was,' he said.

And there it was again. Bang. Like in the comics, she thought a little bit helplessly. Wham, bang, zing, splat.

'Good night, my lord,' she said simply, and he put out a hand and took hers. And winced.

The gesture had been a friendly good-night touch, but as she took his hand in hers and felt its warmth, touched his strength, she also felt something else.

'Ouch,' she said, turning his palm over. And then she saw his palm and she repeated the word with feeling. *'Ouch!'*

'It is a bit,' he confessed, but she was no longer listening.

'Oh, Hamish, your hands. You dope. You blistered them with digging and then to use the axe…'

'We earls aren't wusses.'

'You earls are dopes,' she told him. 'I might have known. Angus was just like you. You know, we had to dress his oxygen canister up in tartan so he could go to his last fair without feeling like a wuss.'

'I don't have an oxygen cylinder,' he said, startled, and she shook her head in disgust.

'Not for want of trying. Hamish, these are awful.'

'Don't say that,' she said uneasily. 'I've been trying to ignore them all day.'

'Right. Ignoring them why? Waiting for your hands to drop off?'

'My hands are not going to drop off.'

'There's ten blisters on this hand,' she said, hauling it closer to get a better look. 'And there's a splinter in this one. And another. You great dope. I'll ring Kirsty.'

'Kirsty?'

'My sister,' she said, exasperated. 'This needs medical attention.'

'I'll wash it,' he said, as if granting an enormous concession. 'That'll fix it.'

'It won't fix it.'

'If you tell me how bad it is one more time, I'll cry,' he said, like it was a huge threat, and she blinked and stared up at him in astonishment.

'Really?'

'Um…no.'

'I wouldn't blame you if you did.'

'I won't. I have an aversion to the pastime.'

'Well, don't stick near me, then,' she told him. 'I cry all the time. Just looking at these makes me teary. You great hulking hero.'

'Hero?'

'Axing away with all of these.' She was examining each blister, searching for more splinters, and the thought of him chopping wood, doing it to make the old ladies smile… That's why he'd done it, she thought. She'd thought he'd done it because it had seemed fun but now, looking at these hands, she thought he'd done it because that's what she'd asked him to do. Create a diversion from Angus's death. Give the locals something else to think about it. He'd eaten scones, he'd chopped wood, he'd placed every eye on him and he'd made people smile.

'Please, don't cry.' He sounded so scared that she stared up at him in even more bewilderment. His face was set, and he was backing away. But she had hold of his hand and she wasn't letting him go anywhere. He was a dope but he was a great, gorgeous dope and he'd done this because she'd asked him to. Therefore—at great personal sacrifice—she'd choke back tears and be businesslike.

'I'm not crying,' she said, trying to sound exasperated and not emotional. 'Sit.'

'Sit?'

'I'll clean them and I'll pull the splinters out. And then I'll put on iodine and we'll see how much of a man you are. You don't cry, huh? Iodine on these will be a real truth test. Iodine would make an onion howl all by itself.'

So he sat in the old rocking chair in front of the range, his free hand soaking in a bowl of soapy water she'd rested on his kilted knees while she carefully examined each blister, cleaned it, lifted out tiny shards of wood with a pair of tweezers—and then anointed each one with iodine.

'You should have a bullet to bite on,' she told him, and he looked down at her mop of auburn curls and thought he wasn't even near yelling. He was hardly thinking about pain.

She was intent on his hand. She was so…simple, he thought, but maybe that wasn't the word. She'd changed from the clothes she'd worn at the fair. Now she was wearing a pair of shorts and a faded T-shirt that was a little too tight. Her legs and her feet were bare. She was wearing no make-up. Her hair was falling forward, stopping him seeing what she was doing with his hand but at the same time distracting him nicely.

She smelt of some citrusy soap, he thought. She'd probably showered when she'd come home from the fair. Maybe she and Rosie had bathed together and the vision of her bathing her baby was suddenly....

Whew. It was just as well Marcia was coming, he thought. A man could get himself into dangerous territory here.

And why wouldn't a man want to?

The thought was so far out of left field that he blinked and almost pulled his hand away. She felt the tug and looked up in concern, all huge eyes and tousled hair and...and Susie.

'I'm trying hard not to hurt you.'

'You're not hurting me.'

'Tell me about your job,' she said, turning her attention back to the splinters as if it was important that she look at anything but him. As maybe it was.

'My job?'

'You're a financier.'

'Mmm.'

'You love being a financier?'

'I guess.' Did he? He wasn't sure.

'I've been trying to imagine why,' she told him. 'I get such a kick out of planting something and watching it grow. Do you see schemes through to the end? Like if someone comes to you and says please can I build a bulldozer factory, can I have some money, does it give you the same thrill? That those bulldozers would never have got built if it hadn't been for you?'

'Um…maybe that's banking,' he said uneasily.

'So you don't do any hands-on supplying of money for doing interesting stuff like building bulldozers.'

'No.'

'So what do you finance?'

'I guess most of my work is taken up with futures broking,' he told her.

'Which is…'

'Figuring out what money is going to be worth in the future and buying and selling on that basis.'

She tweaked out another sliver of wood. Thoughtful. 'So you buy and sell money. It seems a bit odd to me but if it makes you happy…'

Did it make him happy? He'd never thought about it. It seemed such an odd concept that he almost didn't understand the question.

The high-powered finance world was where he'd worked all his adult life. All he knew was wheeling and dealing, the adrenalin rush of vast fiscal deals, the knife edge of knowing it was his brains holding everything in place and if he slipped up…

He thought about his mother's reaction when he'd told her that he'd been made a full equity partner. For once she hadn't cried. She'd closed her eyes and when she'd opened them things had changed.

'Now I can stop worrying,' she'd said.

Full equity partner in one of Manhattan's biggest brokerage firms…well, if that was what it had taken to stop the tears, then great. And he was good at his job. It had earned him a lot, and he had no time to think about anything else.

What else was there to think about but work?

The scent of Susie's hair? That was all he could think about now. That and the feel of her fingers carefully working on his hands. Each blister was being tended with care. It was such a strange sensation. An intimate sensation.

Would Marcia ever tend his blisters?

How would he get blisters around Marcia? He wouldn't. His biggest risk was of repetitive strain injury caused by using his Blackberry too much.

A cold damp something hit the edge of his bare leg and he hauled himself from his reverie and stared down.

Pup.

'Whoops,' Susie said, and laid Hamish's hands carefully on his kilted knees and scooped up the pup. 'That's good timing. Taffy, if you've woken up, you go outside straight away. Hamish, don't touch anything. I'll be back.' And she was gone, whisking the pup out into the gathering dusk.

Don't touch anything.

He sat for a bit, not thinking anything, letting his mind go blank. The sensation was almost extraordinary. When had he last done this?

Simply…stopped.

There was always something to do. Always. Reports to read, e-mail to check, constant analysis. If he didn't keep up then others would get ahead or things could slip by him and, hell, what was the use of being in the heap if you weren't on top?

His laptop was up in his bedroom. He'd connected briefly that morning, checking things were OK. He should go up now and see…

It was seven at night. Three in the morning New York time. Not a lot was happening over there right now.

The Japanese market would be online, he decided. The yen had been looking pretty shaky when he'd left. It wouldn't hurt to stay online for a bit and get the feel for…

Susie was out in the garden. With Taffy.

From where he sat he could hear the sea. He could smell the sea.

She'd told him to stay, so he did, sort of. He

walked to the kitchen door and watched while she introduced Taffy to the lawn and explained what was required.

As if the dog could understand.

'There's no hurry,' she was saying. 'I understand it's all a bit strange and new, and there's even more strange and new to come, but we can take our time. Me and Rose will be the constants wherever you are, and we'll always be able to find you a patch of grass. There's not a lot else you need to worry about.'

What about the Dow Jones? Hamish thought, glancing at his watch and wondering what the financial markets had done in the past ten hours. He always needed to worry about the Dow Jones.

But maybe not now. Maybe worrying about financial indices here was…ridiculous.

Susie was kneeling on the grass. The dopy pup had rolled over onto her back, and Susie was scratching her tummy. She wriggled in delight, her ungainly body squirming with ecstasy on the still sun-warmed ground.

How was she going to cope? Hamish thought. With a baby. With a puppy. She had a lot to worry about. She should be worrying about it right now!

She wasn't worrying. She lay on the grass herself and the puppy climbed on top of her. The last flickers of light from the tangerine sunset were soft on her face. She was giggling as the puppy tried to lick her cheek. From behind he could hear Rose chirping as she woke from what he presumed was a very late afternoon nap. Susie would never get her daughter to sleep tonight.

But she didn't care, he thought. She had no sense of order. He remembered his mother if dinner was five minutes late. She'd be almost apoplectic with anxiety.

He thought of Marcia if things didn't run to plan. What would Marcia do if he gave her a puppy?

Marcia would give the puppy right back. And as for a baby…

Marcia letting a baby having an afternoon nap at this hour? Marcia having a baby?

The idea was so ridiculous that he grinned and Susie looked over and saw him grinning and said, 'What?'

'What yourself?'

'You're laughing at me.'

'I'm laughing at your puppy. There's a difference. Rose is awake.'

'Goody.' She scrambled to her feet, put the puppy down and made to go indoors. 'She went to sleep on the way home and wouldn't wake up. She'll be so hungry. I almost woke her but then I remembered there's an English comedy show I like on TV late tonight, and it's the best fun watching it with Rose.'

Then as he blinked, trying to reconcile late-night comedy and a fourteen-month-old toddler, she hesitated. As she'd started toward the door Taffy had followed.

'You haven't done what you need to do,' she told the puppy, and pointed to the grass. 'Duty first.'

The puppy looked up at her new mistress with adoration, and wagged her tail.

'Stay here with her while I fetch Rose,' Susie ordered Hamish, and he nodded and put a foot out to stop Taffy following her mistress.

Taffy sat down and howled.

They both looked at Taffy. Taffy looked at both of them, opened her jaws and howled even longer.

'Whoops,' Susie said. 'What have I let myself in for?'

'Give her back,' Hamish told her.

'What?'

'You don't have to keep her.'

She snatched Taffy up and glared. 'What a thing to say. Don't listen, sweetheart. You're mine. We're a family. I don't mind the odd howl. It's an excellent howl and it's all your very own. I wonder if you'll like my TV programme, too.'

This was seriously weird. There were all sorts of things happening inside Hamish that he had no idea what to do with.

'You can't be a family to that…that.'

'That gorgeous pup? I can be a family with whoever I want,' she snapped, hauling herself up to her full five feet four inches and glaring. 'Taffy needs me out here. Can you fetch Rose?'

'What, get her from her cot?'

'That's the plan.'

'Just walk in and pick her up?'

'You earls have great courage,' she said, obviously trying not to sound sarcastic. 'If you pick her up under the armpits and close your palms, it won't even hurt your blisters.'

It wasn't his blisters he was afraid of. 'I can't pick up a baby.'

'Don't be ridiculous. Get in there.'

'Woof,' said Taffy.

He stared at the pair of them and they stared back, challenging.

He could do this. Right. *You earls have great courage…*

Right.

He strode into the house, followed the sound of Rosie's increased indignation and pushed open the door to Susie's and Rosie's shared bedroom. And paused in astonishment.

The bed was vast, a great four-poster with mounds of eiderdowns and more mounds of cushions. There were pinks and purples and almost crimsons and gold. It was an amazing bed.

And the walls…

Deirdre's kitsch ornaments had been taken down, and Susie had covered the walls with prints—not expensive artwork but prints she'd obviously ordered because they appealed.

There were all sorts of prints.

Tree ferns taken from strange angles. Waterfalls. Rock formations. That was one wall.

Another wall was the sea—vast curling waves, surfers doing all sorts of incredible twisting turns, shots of foam, a single rock pool, a tiny minnow against a vast pier pile…

The third was people. Grins. People smiling. These weren't people she knew. Ancient Tibetan grandmothers with gap-toothed grins. Old men smiling at each other in friendship. A group of kids in Scout uniform, smiling in unison.

And the last wall was photographs blown up. Susie as a kid, he thought, looking at twins cavorting on a beach. Photographs of a man who was obviously Rory. A couple in love. He looked at them smiling at each other, and felt a twist of…

No. Don't look. You don't need to feel like this.

It was dumb to put such photographs up, he thought. This was as kitsch as Deirdre's efforts.

But then he thought, No, it's not. He thought of his apartment back in Manhattan, and Marcia's, planned by the same minimalist decorator who'd recoil in horror if she saw this. But this sort of worked. It was a huge collage of life, of living, of all Susie held dear.

An indignant yell brought him back to earth. In the centre of the room was that which Susie held dearest. The toddler was beaming as she saw she'd caught his attention. She was holding her hands out and saying, 'Up.'

'Hi,' he said weakly, and she bounced and grinned and held her hands higher.

'Up, up, up.'

He could do this. He put his hands under her arms and gingerly raised her.

She giggled and pointed to the bed. 'Dappy,' she said.

Dappy. He thought about it. Then he realised what she meant. Um, no.

He made to carry her—holding her at arm's length—out the door, out to her mother, but her yell became urgent. He had her agenda wrong.

'Dappy, dappy, dappy.'

You earls have great courage.

'Where are your diapers?' he asked, and she pointed an imperious finger to the pile on a side table. Under the Tibetan grandmas.

'Dappy.'

OK. He set Rose down on the floor but she yelled in indignation. Her routine was obviously to be followed to the letter.

'Bed,' she said, and pointed.

'Give me a break,' he said weakly, but he was a man under orders. He tossed a diaper across to the bed, then lifted Rose and set her down on the eiderdown. She almost disappeared in its vastness.

She giggled and kicked her feet, squirming away from him and burrowing under the cushions. This was obviously a game, played whenever she woke up.

The bed smelt like Susie.

The room smelt like Susie.

Rose lifted a cushion, grinned at him, chortled and pulled the pillow back over her head again. He considered, then put a finger on the small of her back and tickled.

Shrieks of laughter and she squirmed deeper. Right under the quilt.

He put his head under the quilt and said, 'Boo.'

'Dappy,' she said, and pushed the quilt away, lay flat and waited. 'Boo' was obviously the magic word.

And he performed magic as well. Hamish Douglas, corporate financier, ninth Earl of Loganaich, successfully changed a diaper.

'Like climbing Annapurna One,' he told himself, setting Rose on the floor, carrying the used diaper into the bathroom in triumph and thinking of the world's second most difficult climb. 'A soggy diaper. A soiled diaper represents Everest.'

Then as Rose looked thoughtful he tossed the diaper into the wastebin and dived on the toddler to take her out to her mother before she could send him up his second mountain.

He wasn't ready for Everest yet.

Susie was still waiting for Taffy to perform. She was sitting on a garden seat, watching the dark settle over the garden, simply…waiting.

Hamish delivered her daughter, Rose squirmed down onto the grass and she and Taffy proceeded to investigate each other.

'Aren't you going to make her dinner?' Hamish asked, and Susie smiled down at her puppy and her daughter and shook her head.

'No one's in a hurry.'

It was such a strange concept that Hamish blinked.

'You want a seat?' Susie wriggled sideways, making room on the bench.

Why would he sit down? Just to sit?

'Maybe I'll work on the path.'

'With those hands? Are you out of your mind?'

'We earls have great courage.'

'You earls need a straitjacket if you work with hands like those. Just stop, Hamish. Rest.'

He sat. Gingerly. It felt weird.

'Thank you for today,' she said gently, and he felt even more weird.

'Why…?'

'You've made today happy for a lot of people. Just by being here.'

'Just by exposing my knees?'

'A thing of beauty is a joy for ever,' she said serenely, and he choked.

'Right.'

'Honest, Hamish.' Her hand came out to touch his arm. Lightly resting. There was no pressure but the feel of her fingers on his arm was almost his undoing. That and the warmth of the night, the soft hush of the sea, the weird domesticity of pup and baby playing at their feet…

'You were wonderful,' she said, and suddenly she twisted so she could kiss him. Lightly. It was a kiss of thanks. No more than that. A feather kiss.

Except…it wasn't.

People kissed all the time, Hamish thought. They kissed in greeting, and farewell, or as had just happened, to say thank you. It meant nothing. There was no reason to think that a twenty-thousand-volt electric charge had just cut off every other circuit in his body.

Why?

There was no reason, he thought, dazed.

Or was it because Susie was a thousand light years away from any other woman he'd ever dated? She was a thousand light years from Marcia. In her faded shorts and T-shirt and nothing else, nothing to attract, nothing at all, she smelt…she felt…

Soft and delicious and absolutely, imperatively desirable.

It was just the day, he thought, hauling back in shock and dazed wonder. It had been a day totally out of his experience, and he was floundering here because he'd never met anyone like this before, and there were probably thousands of women who were like this but he'd just never met them, and he was out of his comfort zone, and…

'Hey, Hamish, I'm not planning on jumping you,' Susie said, and he jerked back to reality. To Susie staring at him with eyes that were bemused—and maybe also a little hurt.

'I know. It's just…I'm engaged to Marcia.'

Maybe that had been the wrong thing to say.

'I know you're engaged to Marcia,' she said with asperity. 'You really do think I'm planning on jumping you. Just because I'm a widow.'

'No.'

'You do,' she said, and there was no disguising the anger now. She rose and stood, glaring at him with her hands on her hips, vibrating with fury. 'If your colleague in the next office said goodbye, have a good vacation, and kissed you, what would you have thought?'

'Nothing.' Of course not. It was what had happened. 'Hey, Hamish is off on a vacation, can you believe that? 'Bye, Hamish, take care.' Kiss.

It meant nothing. But he had to stop thinking sideways. Susie was in temper-on mode.

'But because I'm a widow, everyone looks at me like I'm encroaching. Like I'm just planning how to get the next man into my bed. Like I'm every married woman's worst enemy. Even you. It's so unfair. I loved Rory like I've never loved anyone. I'm not in the market for another relationship, and hauling Marcia over here just to protect yourself... Don't think I don't realise what you're doing, Hamish Douglas. There was no inkling from you that Marcia would be coming until everyone looked at us like a couple. Then you started looking like a rabbit caught in headlights. It's just so dumb. Dumb, dumb, dumb.' She swooped down and lifted Rose into her arms.

'Come on, sweetheart. We'll go make you some dinner and leave his Lordship here in solitary splendour. In the knowledge that his virtue can remain intact for his precious Marcia. But know that even if there were a million Marcias—or do I mean if there weren't any?—there's no way I'm interested in you, Hamish Douglas, Not the least little bit. Not one skerrick. You leave me as cold as a flat, dead fish.'

She turned and wheeled into the house. Hamish was left starting after her.

Taffy looked at up him, doubtful.

'I'd follow,' he told the pup. 'I'm a flat, dead fish.'

Taffy hesitated a bit more but then as Hamish remained unmoving she obviously decided that maybe Hamish was right. Flat, dead fish were a bit unappetising.

He followed Susie.

There was absolute silence. Even the hush of the sea was fading.

Nothing.

A flat, dead fish.

He should go check his e-mail. He should—

There was a groan from the house and Susie's head appeared at the kitchen window.

'Thanks for sending Taffy inside,' she snapped. 'She's done her business in the hallway. Over to you, your Lordship.'

Great. He rose. *We earls have great courage.*

Even flat, dead fish had their uses.

CHAPTER SEVEN

WHAT followed were a couple of very strained days. Susie and Hamish skirted each other with extreme caution.

They spent the mornings at the beach—well, why wouldn't they as the beach was there and gorgeous? Taffy loved it. Rose loved it. Hamish loved it. He admitted that to himself but, hell, it was a strain. Susie was a small indignant puff of offence and she treated the beach as if they'd put a fence down the middle, with strictly segregated His and Hers zones. When he offered to take care of Rose to give her time to swim she accepted graciously—as if she was granting him a favour—but she flounced out to sea and flounced back, and ignored him in the interim.

'I didn't mean to offend you,' he told her.

'You didn't offend me. You merely implied I saw you as husband material. As nothing could be further from the truth, I believe we need to keep things formal.'

Right. Formal.

By the time Marcia arrived on Monday evening he was almost relieved. Anything to break the formality.

Marcia arrived with Jake. Jake had gone up to Sydney for a one-day pain management conference, and as the times fitted perfectly, he'd offered to collect Marcia from the airport and bring her down. So at eight on Monday night Hamish strolled out to the castle forecourt to greet his fiancée.

'Hi, sweetheart,' he said as she emerged from Jake's truck. He hugged her elegantly suited body close and kissed her—so deeply that he caught her by surprise. When the kiss ended she pulled back and looked astonished.

'Wow,' she said, touching her lips like they were bruised. 'It's only been a few days.'

'I've missed you.'

'Is the widow watching?'

The widow. It took him a minute to catch that but realised, of course, Marcia would think he was playing for an audience. Since he'd implied...

'Have you warned Marcia about our Susie?' Jake asked, sounding interested, and Hamish grimaced.

'I haven't told Marcia anything.'

'Only that the whole place is expecting you to marry her,' Marcia said smoothly. 'You might as well say it like it is, sweetheart. Keep things out in the open so there's no misunderstanding.'

'No misunderstanding,' Jake said blankly. 'Right.'

'Um…good trip?' Hamish said, feeling desperate. 'Have you two found lots to talk about?'

'I slept all the way,' Marcia said. She turned to Jake and gave him her loveliest smile, which was only slightly patronising. 'Thank you so much. I'm afraid I was very boring.'

'Not at all,' Jake told her politely. 'I'll leave you to your Hamish, then, shall I?'

'That would be kind.' Peasantry dismissed.

'Right, then,' Jake said, and with a wry grin he folded his long body back into the driver's seat of his battered Land Cruiser, gave a salute of acknowledgement and left.

'That was a bit brusque,' Hamish said, frowning as Jake backed out of the forecourt. 'Did you two not find anything to talk about at all?'

'Honestly, darling, he's a family doctor. I don't even have any bunions to talk about.'

'I guess not.'

Marcia was out of her territory, he thought, suppressing irritation. She wasn't normally this brittle. Maybe she was just better among her own kind.

He was her kind, he remembered. This was the

woman he intended marrying. He loved her cool, sophisticated humour. She was so intelligent…

'So where's the widow?' she asked.

'Inside. I'll take you to meet her.'

But she hung back, taking a moment to absorb the whole moonlit scene, the fairy-tale castle, the mountains behind, the fabulous coastline.

'This will sell for a mint,' she breathed. 'Oh, Hamish, imagine this in *Vogue Traveller.* Your own little Scottish castle without all those horrid fogs and bogs and midges of Scotland.'

'There's nothing wrong with Scotland,' he said, and startled himself by how fervent he sounded.

'You've never been to Scotland.'

'No, but I'm a direct descendant…'

She gave a peal of laughter and tucked her hand into his arm. 'You've become the Lord of Loganaich,' she said affectionately. 'My very own earl, defending the land of his forebears. Any minute now you'll be up on the turrets playing your bagpipes.'

He grinned, relaxing a little. 'I do wear a mean kilt.'

'This I have to see.'

'You need to meet Susie first.'

'The widow. OK, let's get the scary part over and then get down to the fun part. This place sounded good on paper but in reality… Wow! Let's figure what this pile is really worth!'

* * *

The meeting between Susie and Marcia was not an unqualified success. Susie was in the kitchen, cleaning up. She greeted Marcia with cautious courtesy. Marcia responded in kind—while clinging to Hamish's arm with proprietorial affection—and then Susie excused herself.

'There's steak in the fridge, Hamish, if Marcia's hungry. I'd cook it but—'

'But I do a better steak than you do,' Hamish told her, smiling encouragingly. Wishing she didn't look so tense. Wishing he hadn't told Marcia there was a problem.

Wishing Marcia wasn't clinging quite so close.

'I'll go to bed, then,' Susie said, and Marcia glanced at her watch, astonished.

'It's only eight.'

'Susie's recovering from injuries,' Hamish said, and then wished he hadn't said that as well, as Susie flashed him a look of anger.

'I'm not recovering from injuries. I'm recovered from injuries.'

'You limp,' Marcia pointed out, and Susie glowered a bit and limped her way past them.

'So I do,' she agreed. 'It's my own little idiosyncrasy. But I like it. I'm going to bed to read a good romance novel and I don't intend to recover at all.

Hamish, you need to show Marcia through the castle. I'll bet she's interested in your inventory. And when you've finished... Marcia, could you let me know when this hotel assessor's expected, as I need to organise myself to leave? Good night.'

Taffy was snoozing by the stove. Susie scooped her up, glared at the pair of them and left.

'Have I offended her?' Marcia asked, and Hamish sighed.

'I guess...I mean, maybe it wasn't such a good idea to imply there was a problem.'

'What do you mean? Her limp? It's obvious. She can't expect me not to notice.'

That wasn't the problem he'd been talking about. 'Never mind. Are you hungry?'

'Actually, I ate on the way here and I'm very tired. Maybe the widow has a good idea with early bed.' She snuggled back against him. 'Where are we sleeping?'

'I've put you in the bedroom next to mine. Come and I'll show you.'

'Not yours?'

'Um, no. It just seems...'

'A bit mean?' Marcia was struggling to understand. 'Honey, if she really wants you, then the faster she comes to terms with reality the better.'

'It's not like that. It just... Marcia, it seems like

this is Susie's home and I'd like it to stay that way until we leave. I think…separate bedrooms.'

She raised a cool eyebrow. 'Well, that's fine with me. I have a date with my laptop. I've missed so much, trying to get here. There won't be a romance novel for me in bed tonight.'

Hamish slept late. Hours late by his standards. He always woke early in New York to find the latest on the Hang Seng before he went to work. As he was always behind his desk by seven, that meant he went to bed in the small hours and he woke in the small hours. He couldn't remember a time when he'd fallen into bed at ten and slept for more than eight hours.

But here… It was the silence of the place, he thought, or that there was no desk waiting and Jodie had cancelled his imperatives.

He woke and it was already seven-thirty. He lay lazily back on his mound of satin pillows and watched the early morning sunbeams flicker through the floating dreamcatcher Deirdre had hung at the window. Jodie had hung a dreamcatcher on the window of his outer office back in Manhattan. He'd asked her what it was and she'd explained the ludicrous concept in detail.

Susie might not think it ludicrous, he thought. Jodie hadn't. Deirdre obviously hadn't.

He needed Marcia to set him right. She'd be up by now. He should go find her.

But his thoughts kept wandering, snagging different ideas like the dreamcatcher was designed to do.

Where was Jodie was right now? he wondered. Was she making choir stalls with her beloved Nick? He'd miss his secretary when he went back.

When he went back. When he left here.

When he left Susie.

Susie was leaving first.

Maybe he could keep in touch with Susie, he thought. Just to check that she was OK. He'd tell Kirsty and Jake that he'd keep an eye on her.

She'd throw such an offer back in his face, he decided. She didn't need anyone to take care of her.

But he rejected that, too. Of course she needed someone. She thought she was strong enough to care for a baby and a dog and a career. She was planning on working as a landscape gardener again, but anyone could see she had physical problems. Her legs would never hold her up.

He could… He could…

He could do nothing. It was none of his business.

More lying on his satin pillows and thinking. He was head of the clan, he thought. Lord of Loganaich. Laird. It behoved him to care for…

For the relic?

The thought of Susie as a relic was so crazy he laughed and threw off his covers and headed for the shower. He was being dumb. He'd go and find Marcia and show her this crazy castle from stem to stern. They'd smile about how ridiculous it was, they'd talk about practicalities and then she'd bring him up to speed on how the office was coping without him. Marcia was just what he needed.

Right.

Marcia was already in the kitchen. As were Susie and Rose and Taffy. Quite a party. Hamish opened the door and they all turned toward him and glared.

Uh-oh.

A more cowardly man would have retreated. There were obviously issues abroad here. Women's issues?

'We have,' Susie said cautiously, as if she wasn't sure she could trust her voice, 'no soy milk. We have a case of bananas but they're the wrong sort of fruit. Cumquats make the wrong sort of juice and the oranges aren't ripe yet. And Marcia doesn't like the idea of eating strawberries that have been lying on mulch. If you'd warned me Marcia was on a low-carb diet I could have got things in.'

'Low carb's easy,' he said, cautious as Susie and with a wary look at his beloved. 'I mean, steak's low carb.'

'Steak for breakfast?' Marcia shook her head in disbelief. 'Honestly, Hamish, just lend me your car keys and I'll go fetch what I need from the supermarket.'

'It's five miles down the road and it doesn't open until nine,' Hamish said. 'Can't you have toast?'

'The locals eat porridge,' Susie said, lifting a pot onto the range. 'I can recommend it.'

'It's hardly low carb,' Marcia retorted.

'Hey, Marcia, it's hardly a hotel yet,' Hamish said uneasily. 'It wouldn't hurt to break your diet for a morning.'

'I'd prefer not to break my diet,' Marcia said, but she smiled, ready to be accommodating. 'It's OK, guys. I'm not hungry.'

'You're too thin,' Susie muttered.

'A woman can never be too thin.'

'Yeah, you'd know,' Susie muttered, and banged her pan on the range. Then she took a grip. 'Sorry. That sort of just came out. I was too thin for a while and it's scary.'

'I have no intention of heading down the eating disorder road,' Marcia said. 'I have too much control.'

'I'm sure you have,' Susie said, but the eyes she turned on Hamish were suddenly bleak. 'I've made a big pot of porridge. Do you want some?'

'Yes, please.' It was the least a man could do in the circumstances, he thought, but then he saw the sudden gleam behind Susie's eyes and thought, Uh-oh.

'A porridge-eating laird,' she said thoughtfully. 'Finally.'

'I'm back on toast tomorrow.'

'I'm sure you are.' There was definitely laughter there now. She was like a chameleon, he thought. Swinging from happy to sad and back again.

He didn't want her to be sad. Had she been too thin? When? After Rory's death? Hell, he hated to think of what she'd been through.

'Have you been working up in your bedroom?' Marcia asked, and he blinked.

'Um…yeah.'

'Did you see the Euro dropped almost two cents against the greenback overnight?'

'And Taffy slept till dawn without howling once,' Susie added. 'It has indeed been a busy night.'

He couldn't keep up with this conversation. He gave up and sat, and Susie placed a bowl of porridge in front of him. He ladled honey on top, and cream, and he sprinkled it with cinnamon, as he'd seen Susie do with hers every morning, while Marcia looked on with distaste.

'Don't look,' he told her. 'Have a coffee.'

'At least there's a decent coffee-maker,' she

conceded. 'Though where you get good beans…you know, that'll drive down the price of this place as a hotel. You won't be able to source reasonable foodstuffs.'

'I'm eating my porridge out in the garden,' Susie announced, a little too loudly. She lifted Rose's high chair—with Rose in it—and hoisted it toward the door.

'Let me help,' Hamish said, getting to his feet, but Susie was already outside.

'Thanks, but I'm fine on my own.'

'You will let me help you down to the beach later on?'

She hesitated, and he could see her reluctance to accept help warring with her huge desire to swim.

'Thank you,' she muttered. 'That would be… nice.' She carried Rose further out, then dived back for her porridge.

'Susie…' Marcia started, but Susie was back out the door.

'I can't leave Rose in her high chair alone.'

'I just thought you might be interested…'

'In what?'

'I've been in touch with the hotel assessors,' she said. 'They'll arrive tomorrow. Can you make yourself available?'

Susie hardly paused. She was carrying her bowl

of porridge, walking out the door with Taffy following loyally behind.

'Of course,' she said with dignity over her shoulder. 'I promised. And after that I'll go home.'

Marcia took her Blackberry to the beach. 'Hey, there's a signal here,' she announced, and was content. She lay in her gorgeous bikini and communed with her other world.

As he should, too, Hamish thought, but he was busy watching Susie. He'd swum less than usual this morning, coming back to the towels to keep Marcia company—but Marcia didn't need company. She never did. She was going to make an excellent partner, he decided as he sat next to her beautifully salon-tanned body. She was gorgeous, she was clever and she was totally independent.

She was just what he needed.

Susie was at the other end of the beach—of course. She was sitting in the shallows with Rose. Rose was perched on her mother's knees, kicking out at each approaching wave, as if by kicking it she could stop it coming.

Taffy was barking hysterically at incoming waves, barking until the wave was almost on her then putting her tail between her legs and scooting up the beach just in front of the white water. Then she barked in triumph as the wave retreated—only to have it all happen again.

Hamish discovered he was grinning as he watched them.

But they weren't perfect.

Marcia was perfect.

What was he about, making comparisons?

'I'll go over and give Susie a break from child-minding so she can have a swim,' he told Marcia, and she raised her eyebrows in amused query.

'You? Look after a baby?'

'I can change a diaper,' he said, almost defiantly, and her smile widened.

'If I were you I'd never put that on your curriculum vitae. It's not the sort of ability that'll get you a job in our world.'

Our world. He looked down at her Blackberry. Right.

'Do you want help childminding?' she asked, and it was time for his brows to hike.

'You're kidding.'

She smiled. 'You're right. I'm kidding. But if it's something I need to do for a smooth transition…'

She'd do whatever it took to build a solid financial future, he thought. Wise woman.

'Go back to your wheeling and dealing,' he told her. 'Babysitting's not an occupation I plan on doing any more in my life, but you're right. By doing it now I'm making things smoother for Susie.'

'Not for you?'

'Only in that…' He paused. Only in that it made Susie happier? Only in that it let Susie have one of her last swims in this place? He couldn't think how to finish his sentence.

'Go do it, Nanny Douglas,' Marcia told him, deciding to be amused. 'And be careful when you stand up. I don't want sand in my keypad.'

Then it was his turn to sit in the shallows and entertain Rose while Taffy barked and Susie swam. Not that Rose needed to be entertained. She'd happily kick waves for the rest of her life, he thought.

Were there waves where she was going?

He didn't know.

He couldn't care.

Susie disappeared as soon as they got back from the beach, retreating to the bedroom with a couple of vast suitcases she'd retrieved from the box room and a carton of garbage bags. They hardly saw her for the rest of the day.

'I'm so pleased she's being sensible,' Marcia told him. 'There was hardly any need for me to come. I don't think she's the least bit interested in you.'

'No.'

'You know, it really is the most beautiful place,' she said. They'd finished a fairly strained dinner—fish and chips that Hamish had gone into Dolphin Bay to fetch, and a bowl of steamed vegetables for Marcia—and now they were sitting on the balcony, looking out at the bay in the fading light. 'It seems a shame to sell it straight away.'

'What else would I do with it?' Hamish said shortly. He'd thought this through. Sure, this was a financial windfall, and realistically he didn't need the interest that he'd get from its sale. He'd thought that maybe he could leave Susie here as indefinite caretaker but he'd known instinctively that she'd refuse such an offer. It was a dumb idea anyway. It'd leave her in limbo, his indefinite pensioner. She needed to move on. 'You surely aren't suggesting we live here?'

'No, but I've been thinking that doing some capital improvements before we put it on the market might get us a better price,' Marcia told him. 'I'll need to talk to the assessor tomorrow but… Come and see what I mean.'

'What—?'

'Just come and see. Why no one's thought of this before this is beyond me.'

She led the way downstairs out to Susie's vegetable garden, with Hamish following feeling bemused. Marcia had only been here for twenty-four hours, yet she already seemed proprietorial. She was leading him though his very own castle.

He shouldn't mind. He didn't. It was just…

It was just that this was Susie's place, he thought, but that was dumb. But when he emerged to the twilight and saw Susie's garden he stopped thinking his idea was dumb and decided that it was right. It certainly seemed Susie's place. Her garden was fabulous.

He had no illusions as to who'd done the work here. For the last twelve months, as Angus's health had slowly deteriorated, Susie must have thrown her heart and soul into caring for this place. Her vegetable garden could feed a small army. If this was turned into a hotel the chef would never have to go near a greengrocer.

But Marcia wasn't interested in the garden. She was striding purposefully toward the conservatory. She pushed open the doors and flicked the light, then swore as the light didn't work. It was dusk and the place was still lovely—smelling of ripening oranges and overripe cumquats and the rich loam that Susie had been using to pot seedlings. The lack of light made it seem more beautiful.

'This is what I brought you to see,' Marcia said, in the same voice she used when she produced a contract that was hugely advantageous to the firm— and to her. 'It's fabulous.'

'It is,' Hamish said, walking forward and touching the same branch of hanging cumquats Susie had touched the first day he'd met her. Was it his imagination or could he sense her here? This place seemed almost an extension of her.

'We need to take the end wall out so we can get machinery in,' Marcia was saying, and he blinked.

'Pardon?'

'It's great. Can't you see it?'

'See what?'

'The view from the end wall is right down to the sea. The tourists this place will attract will spend most of their time right here.'

'Why?'

'A swimming pool,' she said with exaggerated impatience. 'I thought about it this morning while I was at the beach. The beach is lovely but most tourists don't want to spend much time there.'

'Why not?'

'The sand gets into your Blackberry, for one thing,' she said, getting even more exasperated. 'Hamish, when we went to Bermuda last year, did we spend any time at the beach?'

'We were there at a conference.'

'Exactly. We had things to do. There was a beach but did we use it?'

There had been a beach, Hamish remembered.

He thought back to an intense four days of business dealings. He remembered watching the sun rise from his hotel room, watching the view, watching people stroll on the beach…and then fitting in a fast fifteen minutes in the hotel pool before breakfast.

'We're the clientele we'll attract,' Marcia said. 'People who appreciate what luxury really is. Anyway, I'm thinking we need to heave out every bit of kitsch before we put this place on the market. And I'm also thinking that we should dig a pool into this building. Honestly, Hamish, buyers have no imagination. Did you see the potential of this place as a swimming pool?'

'No.'

'There you go, then,' she said triumphantly. 'I'll talk it through with the assessor tomorrow but I think you should hold selling off a little longer while we transform this place.' She hesitated. 'I don't suppose we could persuade the widow to stay as a transitional caretaker.'

'I suspect we don't have a hope.'

She shrugged. 'Well, there's others. Maybe we need someone a bit more level-headed anyway.' There was a beep from her belt and she lifted her Blackberry and peered at the lit screen. 'Charles,' she said in satisfaction. 'He has some figures I need. If you'll excuse me, darling… Walk through to the

end and see if I'm right. A swimming pool and a bar
with a view to die for. Our tourists wouldn't have
to move. I suspect the pool could double our price.'

And she was off, leaving him to his thoughts.

His thoughts...

He didn't have any thoughts, he decided. He was
a blank. He fingered his cumquat some more and
thought it was a great smell. It was a great place.

A luxury swimming pool? Maybe they'd have a
few of these orange trees in tubs round the side...

'You'd really chop down all Angus's orange trees?'

Susie's muted voice was so unexpected that his
heart forgot to take a beat. He stilled, trying to think
what to say, and she came out of the shadows and
stood right before him. Still in the plain faded shorts
and T-shirt he was starting to get to know. Still with
bare feet. Her hair was tousled and there was a
smudge of dirt on her forehead.

'I didn't know you were here,' he managed, when
he got his breath back.

'I've been planting out seedlings into bigger pots.
I was intending to plant them straight into the vegetable garden but now I'm leaving I'll need to find
other homes for them. Am I supposed to apologise?'

He was still discomfited. 'You could have told us
you were here.'

'I could have come out of the dark and said I

heard every word? That's what I'm doing now. I didn't mean to eavesdrop but what Marcia was saying…it made me feel…' She paused. 'But, of course, it's none of my business.'

'No.' There was no way to dress this up, he decided, shoving his sense of disquiet aside. If he was going to sell this place he couldn't be looking over his shoulder all the time, wondering what Susie was thinking.

'Angus was so proud of his oranges,' she said wistfully, and he braced himself.

'Someone else will be proud of a swimming pool.'

'It sounds like Marcia will be proud.'

'That's right. Though it's a business proposition. She'll be pleased if it means we get a good price for this place.'

'But…' She paused. 'If you sell the castle, doesn't the money go into trust?'

'It does.' He'd looked into this. It was a complex inheritance, where the castle was a part of the entailed estate to be handed down to the inheriting earl. Generation after generation. It had been made complex by the burning of the original castle, meaning the capital had been moved here. The trustees would allow sale, but the proceeds would return to the trust.

But he'd earn interest on a very sizeable sum.

'Will you and Marcia have children?' she asked. 'To inherit?'

'I…' How to answer that? He thought about it and decided he didn't have to. 'I have no idea.'

'It's just…would your son prefer to inherit a castle or a heap of depreciating money?'

'Hell, Susie…'

'But that's easy, isn't it?' she said sadly. 'That's the choice you made and you've made it really fast.'

'What would I do with this place if I kept it?'

'You could think laterally,' she said with sudden asperity. 'Instead of thinking what's the best way to make money from this place. You're not exactly needy.'

'No, but—'

'But you'll chop down these gorgeous orange trees. Do you know, it's five hundred miles to the nearest place you can grow oranges from here? The locals here eat Angus's oranges all winter. We have the best vitamin C intake per capita of any place in the country.'

'Gee,' he said blankly, and she glared at him in the dusk. He couldn't see the glare, he thought, but he could feel it.

'You don't care.'

'Susie, we both need to move on.'

'I am moving on,' she said with irritation. 'You're

not moving anywhere, as far as I can see. You're taking your money and bolting back to your safe hole in Manhattan. What is it with you and money? Why is it so important?'

'Money's important to everyone.'

'To provide necessities, yes,' she snapped. 'Even enough to buy the odd luxury when you feel inclined. But Marcia says what you earn is way out of that league.'

'Marcia has no right—'

'And neither do I.' She turned her back on him, lifting a branch of cumquats, heavy with fruit. She started plucking the fruit from the loaded branch, making a pile on the bench beside her. 'OK. I'll butt out of what's not my business.'

'What are you doing?'

'I'm picking your cumquats,' she snapped again. 'What does it look like?'

'What for?' They were hardly edible. He'd tried one yesterday. They looked fabulous, like tiny mandarins, lush and filled with juice, but the first bite had seen him recoil.

'They're great for marmalade.'

'You can't cook.'

'I intend to learn,' she said with dignity. 'I'm leaving here the day after tomorrow and I'm taking some of Angus's cumquat marmalade with me.'

'So you'll learn and do it tomorrow.'

'Why not?'

She was fearless, he thought. A vision of Susie down in the cove was suddenly in his head, a scarred, limping woman, diving full on into the white water and heading for the outer reaches of the cove. Her body strong and sure and determined.

She'd succeed in her landscaping business, he thought. Clients would be lucky to get her. She was so...

So...

He picked a couple cumquats to add to her pile and her body grew stiffer. She had her back to him—he was of no importance to her.

'Thanks, but I can do this myself.'

'You just said you can't cook marmalade.'

'Neither can you.'

'But I have a connection to the Internet. I bet we could find a recipe.'

'So you'll find a recipe,' she said, and then decided maybe she was being a bit grumpy. 'Thank you. I'll do them tomorrow.'

'The assessor's coming tomorrow.'

'I'll do it after I've talked to him. Or he can talk to me while I stir the marmalade.'

'You need to pack tomorrow.'

'I'm almost packed.'

'You need to swim.'

That made her pause. She hesitated. 'I…'

'You do want to swim on your last day?'

'Of course, but—'

'But you also want to make marmalade. So let's make it now.'

The stiffness of her back had lessened and she turned cautiously around. 'Could we?'

'I'd imagine we need lots of sugar and lots of jars.'

'How do you know?'

'Well, the jars are a given,' he said. 'I'd guess we can't eat more than half a pint of marmalade tonight.'

'I suppose not. We will need jars.'

'And my Aunty Molly used to make jam,' he added. 'So I know we need almost as much sugar as fruit.'

'You used to watch your Aunt Molly cook?'

'I did.' He sounded uncomfortable—he knew he did—and he saw her hesitate as if she'd ask more. She stared at him, searching his face in the dim light, looking for…

He didn't know what she was looking for. And, whatever it was, he knew he didn't want her to find it.

Or he thought he didn't want her to find it.

This conversation was too deep for him. Way too deep. His thoughts were starting to become knotted, and untangling them was impossible.

Chop them off and get on with it, he thought, suddenly savage, and he tugged a cumquat branch toward him and started plucking.

'If we're to finish before midnight, then we start now,' he said, and she waited—and watched—for a moment longer before deciding to play along.

'Rose didn't have an afternoon nap so she's out for the count,' she said. 'So's Taffy. I guess if I go to bed, all I'll do is dream of uprooted orange trees, so I might as well make marmalade.'

'Susie…'

'I know. There's nothing either of us can do about it.' She shrugged. 'I'm being unfair. It's a very nice offer to teach me to make marmalade. I accept with pleasure. Do you think Marcia would like to help?'

CHAPTER EIGHT

MAKING marmalade was a tricky business. It took sugar, cumquats, jars, a recipe, concentration…

They had everything they needed. Deirdre had obviously decided the pantry stores needed to be filled just like a real castle's would be in case of siege—and as sugar didn't seem to have a use-by date and the castle was slightly younger than siege times, they were set.

They found a hoard of a hundred or so empty jars. Hamish downloaded a recipe from the Internet. They had a couple buckets of cumquats.

Which left concentration.

Concentration was harder.

Susie had to remove pips from every cumquat. Hamish was standing right beside her, pipping his own cumquats. The castle was totally silent. Taffy and Rose were fast asleep. Marcia was in her room, online to the other side of the world.

Weren't you supposed to talk companionably as you cooked? Susie thought. Wasn't that in the manual?

He was so big. So male. He was focussed on each individual cumquat pip as if it was his next million-dollar deal.

He was just…just…

She was so…

So what? He didn't know. She was pipping her cumquats in silence, focussed absolutely on the job in hand. She was holding a cumquat half at arm's length, squinting at it so she wouldn't get hit in the eye by juice as she prodded for the pip. Her tongue was out to the side, just a little bit. Intense concentration.

For marmalade.

She'd make a good futures broker, he thought. She was up to approximately cumquat number ninety and she hadn't faltered. Intelligence. Persistence. Great little tongue. Cute nose. Eyes that were so…

'How many more, do you think?' she asked, and he hauled himself back to cumquat duty with a start.

'I'm thinking we've done enough.'

'Right.' She eyed the rest of the cumquats they'd picked—in a bucket on the floor and as yet un-pipped—and shoved them under the bench with her bare toe. Out of sight. Maybe she wouldn't make

such a great futures broker. Maybe she'd make a
better criminal lawyer.

He started to smile but she was waiting, expectant, and he had to haul his thoughts together and
turn to the recipe.

'OK. Put the cumquats and sugar together and
cook until done.

'Just like that?'

'That's what it says.'

'No skill at all. I could do this myself.'

'Would you like to?'

She hesitated. 'No. I wouldn't know what to do
at the end.'

'It says what to do here.'

'Great. You read and I'll stir,' she said. 'OK?'

So she stirred and he read and he stirred and she read
and then they both sat and watched the vast pot of
honey-gold marmalade until finally, finally their test
drop formed a skin and Hamish announced that it was
done.

Their cleaned jars had been sitting in the range for
the duration of the cooking, slowly warming. Hamish
set the jars out and Susie poured and poured and
poured until they had thirty-odd jars of cumquat marmalade lined up on the big kitchen table. They
attached lids, they cleaned up their mess and then they
turned and looked in satisfaction at what they'd done.

All evening they'd worked almost in silence. It wasn't that they'd meant to be silent or that they were uncomfortable with each other, it was simply that words were unnecessary, Susie thought. Now, as she looked at the golden jars, words were even more unnecessary. What they'd done this evening…

She'd take this home with her. Would she eat it? Maybe, but maybe she'd keep one jar.

How long did marmalade last?

How long did love last?

Where had that come from? Dumb thought. She thought of Rory, of standing beside the man she loved, making her wedding vows. She'd thought it would be for ever.

And now she was standing beside this big, kindly man who was Rory's cousin. What she felt for him was…different.

Of course it was different. How could she love Hamish?

How could she not?

But Hamish's thoughts were on practicalities. 'We'll box them up,' he said softly, looking at the pots with the air of a man who'd done a difficult job to his satisfaction. 'If we send them air freight they'll get there as fast as you will. You'll be able to eat Loganaich Castle Marmalade for breakfast every morning.'

'Will you keep some, too?'

'Sure.' He eyed the bucket under the bench. This was a great new splinter skill. How come he'd never thought of doing such a thing? 'Maybe Marcia and I can make some more. But do you want all these?' he asked, suddenly uncertain. 'If you eat porridge for breakfast, then you'll hardly use thirty pots of marmalade.'

'I only eat porridge while I'm here. I never eat porridge while I'm anywhere else.'

He relaxed. 'Very wise. So if Marcia and I make more marmalade we can send it over.'

'Maybe this is enough.'

'It'll last for a good long time.' He grinned, trying to tease her to smile. He liked it when she smiled. The stress lines around her eyes faded, making her seem younger, more carefree. Which was how she should be. 'Every time you eat it you can think that the cumquat trees haven't lived in vain.'

But that was a mistake. As soon as the words were out he knew that he'd committed an error. Reminding her the cumquat trees were doomed.

'I guess I'll remember they've been knocked down.'

'If you want to be miserable you can think that.'

'I don't want to be miserable.'

'Then don't think about it. Move on, Susie.'

'Stop remembering this place?'

'If it makes you emotional, yes.'

'If I stopped thinking about anything that makes me emotional I'd be in for a pretty barren existence.'

'You stay under control that way.'

'Which is important?'

'Of course it's important.' He moved to adjust a marmalade jar which had dared not be in line with the others. Right. He now had thirty perfectly controlled pots.

But moving hot jam jars was a mistake. The jar he moved cracked, like a mini-explosion in the stillness. Maybe the jam had been too hot. Maybe the jar hadn't been heated up enough. Whatever the reason, there was suddenly jam running over the table, spoiling his careful symmetry.

He moved to shift the nearest jars away from the broken one. He lifted one, then swore as the heat seared through the cloth he'd used to lift it. He dropped it—and it cracked like its neighbour.

'I'd just let them settle this among themselves,' Susie said cautiously, eyeing the mess with trepidation. 'This might be an instance where lack of control just has to be accepted.'

'I never—'

'Hamish, if you lift another jar you're risking all-out calamity. I do want some marmalade to take home.'

He eyed the jars. He looked at his burnt fingers. He looked at the mess. 'But if I shifted these—'

Susie grabbed his arm and tugged him over to the sink. 'Leave it,' she ordered. 'Your poor hands.' She plunged his hand under cold water—which did feel better than trying to pick up more marmalade.

'I'll get some burn cream,' she told him but he shook his head.

'It's minor.'

'Then stay under water for a little longer.'

So he did. The marmalade mess stayed untouched. He stayed...out of control?

She was so close. She was holding his arm, forcing his hand to stay under the water. She was so...

'Susie, I'm really sorry about the trees,' he managed.

'You don't have to be sorry about the trees,' she said stiffly.

'If I didn't think what Marcia said made sense... If I didn't realise that any purchaser will do exactly that, chop them down to make way for a pool...'

'Of course,' she said, and sniffed. 'It's totally sensible.' She sniffed again.

'Susie, don't cry.'

'I'm not crying.'

Of course she was crying. Tears were welling up behind her eyes, threatening to fall at any minute.

'OK, we won't do it,' he said desperately—and she dropped his hand in astonishment.

'What?'

'We won't pull down the orange trees.'

'Just because I cried?' she said cautiously.

'I can't bear to see you—'

'You can't bear to see me cry so you'll do what I want.' She thought about it, and suddenly the tears welled up even more. 'I think I need a slice of your inheritance.'

'Susie…'

'Oh, I do.' Tears were streaming down her face now. 'I really do. And I want you to promise me that you'll wear your kilt every third Monday of the month for the rest of your life.'

He was backing off. 'Don't be ridiculous.'

She wiped her face with the back of her hand, turning off the tears like a tap. There was danger-ous mischief glinting behind the tears. 'It's not me who's being ridiculous.'

'You…' He stared at her, stunned. 'You turned on those tears…'

'At will. Neat trick, isn't it?'

'To get what you want?'

'I never cry to get what I want.'

'You just did.'

'Believe it or not, I didn't. If you think I really want you wearing a kilt, driving the women of this world crazy…'

'Then why—?'

'I was teasing, Hamish Douglas. Teasing. You've never heard of the word?'

'By crying.'

'Can we leave the crying alone? It's getting boring.'

This was crazy. She was standing there glaring at him, her eyes still wet, marmalade splashed all over her T-shirt, daring him…daring him…

'I hate you to cry,' he said, sounding dumb, but he didn't know how else to sound.

'So I'm not crying.'

'Susie…'

'What?' she said, almost crossly, and she folded her arms across her breasts and glared.

'You're crazy.'

'Sure. I'm crazy.'

'I want…'

'What do you want, Hamish Douglas?'

What did he want?

The question hung. He glared at her, marmalade-stained and rumpled and angry and not crying, and suddenly…

Suddenly the mist cleared to make way for one dumb plan. There was a myriad of emotions running through his head right now, emotions chasing their respective tails, but the only thing he could think was a stupid, unwise, crazy thought. But once thought, it was not possible to put it aside. It was just there. It had to surface.

It did surface. 'I want to kiss you,' he said.

There was a moment's silence. A long moment's silence. She appeared to consider, jutting her chin slightly forward, slightly belligerent, taking her time to come up with a response.

And finally she did.

'Well, why don't you?' she said.

What was he doing, wanting to kiss Susie?

Was he mad? He was engaged to Marcia. Marcia could walk in at any minute. Even though she wasn't possessive, to find her fiancé kissing another woman might push her a wee bit far.

Might? It would, he thought wildly, searching frantically for the control he so valued.

But his control was nowhere to be found. For Susie was right in front of him. Battered, bruised and beloved Susie.

Beloved? Where had that word come from?

It was just there. As was Susie. She was right in front of him, ready and waiting to be kissed.

* * *

Was she mad? Was she losing her cotton-picking mind? To kiss Hamish… To let him kiss her…

He was engaged to another woman and the day after tomorrow she was leaving here and she'd never see him again in her life.

Which was why…which was why she was proposing to let him kiss her, she decided. For there was a tiny part of her brain that said this was all there was, this moment, this tiny connection that could only last for one fleeting kiss and then be over.

She'd dared him to kiss her. And he'd do just that. Or she certainly hoped he would.

The signs were good.

He had his hands on her waist. He was taking his time, lingering, looking down into her eyes as he drew her against him. He was making sure that he wasn't coercing her. He was making sure that she hadn't made some daft, stupid mistake when she'd agreed to be kissed.

Maybe she had made some daft, stupid mistake but she wasn't admitting it. Not now, when he was so near. So close.

Not when he was so…Hamish.

She was being drawn into him now. She was allowing those big, capable hands—these lovely, strong and battered hands—to pull her against him.

Her breasts were being moulded against the strength of his chest. His hand shifted to cup her chin, tilting her face so her eyes met his.

Things were looking hopeful here. Very hopeful indeed.

He smiled down at her then, a rueful, searching smile that asked more questions than it answered. But there was such tenderness in his look. Such...love?

He was asking a silent question, but she couldn't respond. How could she respond? She gazed help-lessly up at him, and the last vestiges of her laughter faded as she felt her heart lurch sideways. As she felt her heart still, and then start to race as it had almost forgotten it could race.

As she fell. As she tumbled deeper and deeper in love with the man before her.

He was engaged to another woman. She tried to think that but she couldn't.

For it simply couldn't matter. This was too impor-tant, she thought. Hamish intended to kiss her and all she could do was wait...and hope.

Or raise her face a little more to meet his kiss?

Or she could put her hands on his face and draw him down to her.

Definitely. She'd definitely do that.

She could not think of Marcia. Or Rory. There was no room to think of anything or anyone but Hamish.

And his kiss.

She could drown in this kiss.

What was he doing? Kissing a woman who wasn't Marcia?

He was doing what was right, he decided. He was doing what needed to be done.

He was doing what he'd ached to do from the moment he'd first seen Susie.

Oh, the feel of him. The strength, and yet the tenderness. The certainty and yet the hesitation. His mouth plundered hers, yet she knew that if she pulled back— at the slightest hint of pressure—he'd release her.

For this was no man claiming his rights. He was as unsure as she was, as stunned by the strength of feeling between them, and the feeling was unbelievably erotic.

Hamish.

The wild beating of her heart settled and things slipped into place, things that had been out of kilter with her world for so long. She'd thought when Rory had died that she could never love again—but the heart expanded to fit all needs.

She still loved Rory. She'd love him till the day she died but Hamish was a different man, a different love. Her new, wonderful love.

His lips were on hers and he kissed her as she'd ached to be kissed—but she hadn't known there was this ache within her. His lips were tentative, tasting her, feeling her response, feeling by the faint parting of her lips that he was, oh, so welcome.

Hamish.

Maybe she said his name. She didn't know. But his kiss moved, to her nose, gently teasing. To her eyelids, maybe tasting the salt still left by her tears. Her fake tears, produced to mock, but how could she ever mock this man?

His fingers were raking her hair and the sensation was magic. She moaned a little and kissed him back, finding his mouth and claiming it. Tugging his body hard against hers. Curving into him.

She lifted his hand and led it to her breast. Her body was arching against his. It had been almost two long years since she'd been held by a man. She'd loved one man and she'd thought her body could never fit with another but she was wrong, oh, she was gloriously, wonderfully wrong. Her Hamish.

Marcia was nowhere. Marcia simply didn't exist. But this was no betrayal. Susie was no traitorous vixen searching for another woman's man. This had gone way past that. Hamish belonged to no other woman.

Hamish was simply a part of her.

She locked his arms behind him, then lifted her

head to allow him to kiss her as deeply as he wanted. He was tasting her neck, caressing her shoulders with his tongue, and the sensation was so exquisite she thought she must sob with aching pleasure. He slipped his fingers under the soft fabric of her T-shirt, cupping the smooth contours of her breasts, making her moan softly with love and desire. Her hands were locked about his head now, deepening the kiss, deepening, deepening…

There was such want. She hadn't known how alone she was until tonight, when suddenly she was no longer alone.

This man was her man. She knew it at some primeval level she couldn't begin to understand and didn't want to try. The only place in the world that she should ever be at peace was right here, in this man's arms.

Within the arms of the man she truly loved.

She melted into his kiss with abandon, surrendering to the promise of his body. To the feeling that here in his arms anything was possible. She'd never be lonely. She'd never be alone. With Hamish beside her, she could take on the world.

'Susie,' he whispered, and his voice was as unsteady as she felt. 'Dear God, Susie, we can't.'

'We can't…?'

'Make love.'

She froze at that. She froze and thought about it. And reality came flooding back. Awareness of her surroundings.

Awareness of Marcia?

'You mean we can't make love right here in the marmalade.'

'Well…it'd be a bit sticky.'

'I guess.' She pulled away a little, searching to see his face. He looked dazed. Confused. And a little afraid?

'Hey, there's no need to look scared,' she said, and he shook his head, searching for some sort of reality.

'I'm not scared.'

Reality was slamming back fast. Marcia was just upstairs. Hamish was engaged to be married to Marcia. Susie was on her own. The day after tomorrow she was leaving here. Hamish had never said he wanted her. He never said he needed her, yet here she was, wearing her heart on her sleeve, making herself wantonly available.

It couldn't be wanton to kiss the man she loved.

But he didn't love her. She could see. If his eyes reflected hers they'd be full of love and desire and he'd be moving to hug her, moving to claim her.

Instead of which he was staring at her as if she were some sort of witch, capable of casting a spell.

'I didn't mean…'

It needed only that.

'You didn't mean to kiss me?'

'No. Susie, I'm—'

'Engaged to Marcia.' Somehow she made her voice work. 'Of course. I… Look, it's late and we're overtired and—and it was only a good-night kiss after all.'

Liar, she screamed at herself, but he was nodding, though his eyes said he knew as well as she did that it had been no such thing.

'We can't… Susie, Marcia and I are getting married.'

'Of course. And you and I, we'd be impossible. I'm so emotional.'

'Yes,' he said, and there was almost relief in his voice. 'You cry.'

'I do,' she agreed cordially, feeling like crying now, but there was no way she'd cry. Something was being destroyed that had hardly started to be created.

He was still looking at her as if he was afraid. She wanted to scream. She wanted to…

She didn't know what she wanted.

'Of course I cry,' she whispered. 'And you hate crying. I cry all the time, happy and sad, and you can't stand it.' An errant tear rolled down her cheek right then and she wiped it away with anger. He was right—she couldn't even stop crying to save herself.

'I'm not in control,' she admitted. 'Well, that's OK, that's the state of my existence, but for a moment there you weren't in control either. That's what's scaring you, isn't it? You hate it. Well.' She took a long, searing breath, searching frantically for the words to say to finish it. As it had to be finished.

She finally found them, right or not, but the words that had to be said.

'Marcia's upstairs, Hamish. She's your fiancée. She's your future. And I need to check on Taffy. I need to check on Rose. My baby and my puppy. They're my future. And by kissing you I'm just interfering with the way of the world. With the way things have to be from this day forth.'

And before he could say another word she'd turned and fled, out of the kitchen door, back out into the night.

To the vegetable garden? To the conservatory? To the beach?

He couldn't know. There were tears welling in her eyes as she turned away. He couldn't follow.

Should he go to Marcia?

No. He was going to bed. Alone.

CHAPTER NINE

HAMISH went upstairs. He paused by Marcia's door, feeling bad. He knocked lightly and opened the door a crack. Marcia was on the phone, her laptop on her knees, listening intently to the person at the end of the line and staring at her screen. She looked up briefly, saw it was him and blew him a kiss, using the phone instead of fingers.

He wasn't wanted. He closed the door and went to his own room.

Bed.

Sleep?

It was nowhere to be found.

Why had he kissed her? It wasn't as if he could possibly take this any further. It was so unsuitable. Hell, if he married Susie she'd expect…

More than a telephone kiss good-night?

It could never work. He thought of the house he'd grown up in, a house full of hysterical women who had used their emotions to manipulate everyone around them. He'd fought so hard to get away from that. To catapult himself back into it…

Susie wouldn't try to manipulate him.

No, but she couldn't help it. He thought of finishing work and heading home as he usually did, exhausted beyond belief. Collapsing into bed before getting up to do some hard gym work before the next day at the office. How would Susie fit into that?

She'd hate it. He'd hate it. He wouldn't do it.

What would he do instead?

Cut it out, he told himself fiercely into the night. You've spent the last thirty years building up the life you want and to toss it all away for one…one…

It wouldn't be one, he told himself grimly. It'd be more. Susie came with attachments. Rose. Taffy. And more. She'd want more.

And they'd all be emotional. He thought of Taffy sitting on the grass and howling her lungs out because she couldn't get what she wanted.

He grinned.

No. Be serious. Get up and go see what's Marcia working on.

She wouldn't thank him for the interference. She was fiercely independent.

Good. Great.

Life was fine. Go to sleep.

Ha.

He lay for another half-hour or so, listening to the soft hush-hush of the sea. The castle was quiet.

Maybe he could go down and chat to Ernst and Eric.

As if on cue, there was a knock on the door. He didn't have to resort to tin-plated armour, he thought. It'd be Marcia.

'Come in,' he called, and wondered why he felt empty. As though Marcia coming in was going to expose something he didn't want exposed.

But it wasn't Marcia. It was Susie, peering round the door, her face worried in the moonlight.

'Sorry to wake you.'

'You didn't wake me.' He was half out of bed. 'What's wrong?'

'Nothing. I just… Is Taffy here?'

'No.'

'Are you sure?'

'Sure I'm sure.' He frowned. 'My bedroom door was shut when I came upstairs and it's shut now. She couldn't have got in.'

'Oh. Sorry, then.'

'Is she lost?' He was out of bed, crossing the floor, concerned.

'No,' she said, urgently, stopping him in his tracks. 'There's no need for you to come.'

'But if you can't find her…'

'She'll be somewhere sound asleep,' she said.

'This place is too big. We'll find her when she wakes up.'

'But you were looking for her now.'

'I thought I'd take her outside for a piddle before I went to bed. But if she's curled up somewhere I can't find her then I'll have to wait until she wakes up.'

'But…how will you know?'

'I'd imagine Taffy is very good at letting us know where she is when she's hungry,' she said, and he could tell that she was making a huge effort to keep her voice light. Damn, he shouldn't have kissed her. It had brought in all these tensions that he didn't have a clue what to do with. 'You've heard her howl.'

'So I have,' he said. 'But—'

'Go back to bed, Hamish,' she told him.

'Have you checked Marcia's room?'

'Yes. She's been working all the time. She's still working now. I thought… Anyway, if you hear Taffy raising a riot in the wee small hours you'll know what it is. I've warned Marcia.'

'Let me help you find her.'

'No,' she said flatly. 'Please, Hamish, go back to bed.'

'I'd like to help.'

'I don't want you helping.' She hesitated. 'Hamish, I need to be by myself. For the rest of the time I'm here. I'm not sure why what happened tonight happened, but it was dumb and meaningless and I need to back right off. Good night, Hamish.'

She closed the door before he could respond.

He should follow. He could help her search. The thought of Susie searching for her pup in this vast castle left him uneasy.

The thought of Susie doing anything alone left him uneasy.

What had she said? What happened tonight was dumb and meaningless?

Of course it was. They both knew it. Susie was a woman who was controlled by her emotions, and he…well, he knew where emotions belonged.

They didn't belong with Susie!

'Taffy?'

If Hamish heard, he'd come down and help. He mustn't hear. But where was a little dog out here in this huge garden? And the cliffs so near… Taffy had gone over the road to the beach with them so she knew the way. If she'd tried…

There was only one path down to the beach. If she'd become disoriented and ended up on the rocks…

Should she ask Hamish for help?

No. It was as she'd assured him. The night was calm and still and if Taffy needed anything she only had to howl. She'd be snoozing in some obscure corner, and if Hamish came down and helped her search for a puppy who didn't need finding then they might…they might…

She daren't ask Hamish for help. But she needed to find Taffy. She needed to hug her.

She needed to hug someone.

She was bone weary. She had a huge day tomorrow. She should be in bed right now.

Instead, she was just going to walk over the road to the beginning of the path to the beach. Just to check.

'Taffy?'

Seven a.m. Hamish walked into the kitchen, wanting coffee, and Jake was standing at the kitchen bench. Fully clothed. Pouring coffee.

Maybe it was a guy thing but walking in on a man who was fully dressed and looked ready for business—hard, physical business—when wearing boxer shorts and nothing else made Hamish feel a bit like retreating. Fast. He eyed Jake's workmanlike moleskins and heavy-duty shirt with misgivings.

'Morning?' he said cautiously, and Jake swivelled to stare at him.

This wasn't a stare of 'Ooh, who's wearing ancient boxers?'. It was a stare of active dislike.

'Good of you to join us,' he growled.

Hamish glanced at his watch. Seven was not what you'd call a slovenly hour to wake up.

'Are you here for breakfast?'

'We had breakfast an hour ago.'

'We?'

'The girls and I. Kirsty's taken Rose home with her. Susie's searching the bushland behind the garden. I've come back to make a few phone calls. We'll get some back-up.' His voice was so cold each word was practically an icicle 'I want Susie to get some rest. She's not fit to be searching as she's been doing all night.'

His heart stilled.

'Taffy,' he said. 'Hell, she didn't find Taffy.'

If anything, Jake's expression grew colder. 'She said she told you the pup was lost. I thought she must have been mistaken. To let her stay up all night…'

'She didn't stay up all night.'

'Oh, she didn't?' Jake said. 'Fine.'

Hamish stared at Jake in consternation. Jake stared back, as if Hamish was something lower than pond scum.

'I offered to search with her,' Hamish said desperately. 'She said she was sure the pup was somewhere in the castle. That she'd howl when she woke up. She's good at howling.'

'It's not much use howling when you're outside,' Jake muttered, more to himself than to Hamish. 'There's owls hunting at night. If Taffy's attracted one of them... I'm thinking that's what will have happened.'

'She's not outside,' Hamish said flatly. 'She's in the castle.'

'If she was in the castle she'd be howling by now. She's a ten-week-old pup who hasn't been fed for twelve hours.'

'But she was locked in the wet room. Susie put her there when she put Rose down for the night.'

'I gather Marcia used the wet room as a passage early last night,' Jake said. 'It seems she left the door open.'

Hamish thought back. Marcia in the conservatory, fielding phone calls. Marcia walking back to the house to get notes. She'd never notice a pup...

'Where's Marcia now?'

'On the phone to New York. Where do you think?' Jake's voice said Marcia was right there in the pond with Hamish.

'She hasn't seen the pup?'

'What do you think?

Hamish was already backing out the door, heading for some clothes. 'Why are you here?'

'Susie rang Kirsty at dawn.'

'Over a dog?'

'Dumb, isn't it?' Jake said cordially. 'Only a dog. But Susie loves her.'

Hamish closed his eyes. 'I'll get dressed.'

'Right,' Jake said politely, turning back to the phone. 'I'll add you to the search party, shall I?'

'She'll be dead.' Susie stood in the middle of the cove and stared despairingly along the beach. 'She'll have been taken by an owl or an eagle. It's just dumb to keep looking. Dumb, dumb, dumb.'

'Hey, it's not hopeless,' Kirsty told her. She'd left all the kids with her housekeeper and come straight back. 'We have half Dolphin Cove out searching. Jake says the numbers are up to eighty already.'

'Eighty?' Susie hiccuped on a mix of laughter and a sob. 'For one little puppy.'

'Everyone loves you,' Kirsty said solidly. 'There's people coming from everywhere to look.'

'She'll be dead.'

'We'll keep looking until we find her.'

Hamish couldn't believe it. He'd been out in the bushland behind the castle—three hours of combing the rough gullies and hillside, searching in what seemed an increasingly hopeless case. He'd returned to find the kitchen like a military planning area.

'What'd happen if a child was lost?' he asked in amazement.

Kirsty looked up from the table where she was crossing grid lines off a map and gave him a weary smile.

'More of the same.' She shrugged. 'Much more. OK, it might be over the top but the wind's up, which means the fishing fleet can't get out, so the fishermen don't have anything else to do. And everyone knows Susie's leaving tomorrow. We're upset about it already, without this happening.'

'Where's Susie now?'

'I talked her into having a lie down.' She hesitated. 'You know, Susie's not just devastated because of the puppy.'

He thought about it and decided, yes, Kirsty was right, but he knew where Kirsty was headed and there were places there he didn't want to go.

'She'll miss you, too,' he said, deliberately obtuse, and she gave him a long, thoughtful look that reminded him uncomfortably of her twin.

'As you say.'

'Is Jake out searching?'

'Jake had morning surgery. He had to go.'

So Jake was getting on with business. 'Well, someone has some sense.'

Her face stilled at that. Yes, she really was very

like Susie, he thought, and then he thought about what he'd said. Maybe it hadn't been…sensible?

'Sense is a really strange thing,' she said softly. 'Just when you think you have it cornered, it turns into something else. Be careful what you think is sensible, Hamish Douglas. It might just turn around and bite you.'

'Hamish.'

As if on cue, a voice came from the door. He turned and Marcia was standing in the doorway, looking displeased. 'Where have you been?'

'Out searching.' The cell phone in her hand vibrated before he could say any more. She stared at the screen, prioritised and abandoned the caller.

How often was she separated from her phone? Hamish thought, and then he wondered how often he'd been separated from his. Until he'd come here, maybe never.

'You're wanted,' she said briefly, obviously annoyed.

'Susie wants me?'

'By the hotel assessor,' she snapped. 'You knew he was coming this morning. He's in the drawing room. I've shown him around but he wants to talk to you—and to Susie.'

'I'll come,' he said wearily, raking his hand through

his hair. 'But Susie's not to be disturbed.' He turned back to Kirsty. 'Let me know if there's any news.'

Hamish had to focus.

Lachlan Glendinning was the representative of an international realty firm. He'd been valuing a hotel up in Northern Queensland and he'd taken time and considerable trouble to travel to Dolphin Bay. Telling him he couldn't spend time with him because a puppy was missing—especially when Susie had the whole town combing the surrounding estate looking for him—seemed crazy.

But there was no mistaking that outside with the search party was where Hamish wanted to be.

Why? he wondered as he answered Lachlan's endless questions, going over the family history as he knew it. Luckily he'd read many of Angus's family papers so he had the answers to most questions. But his eyes kept straying outside. People were going back and forth under the window. He could see people down on the beach.

'I hear there's a lost dog,' Lachlan said genially. He was smooth and slick and clever, knowing exactly what he was looking for in the real estate market and knowing he'd found it in Loganaich Castle. 'This is quite some community spirit you have here. The town's picturesque, too. I'm thinking we could build this really big.'

'I'm sure you could,' Marcia agreed. She'd abandoned her cell phone and had joined in the conversation with enthusiasm. She and Lachlan spoke the same language.

'I really would like to speak to Mrs Douglas,' Lachlan said regretfully. 'Are you sure there's no way?'

'There's no way.' Hamish rose. 'Marcia, would you like to show Lachlan the grounds? If he's seen all there is here…'

'I've seen enough of the inside,' Lachlan said. 'It's a great interior.' They passed into the hall and he poked at Ernst with his gold-embellished fountain pen. 'Though these guys will have to go. I know where we can get some real ones.'

'Ernst and Eric are coming home with me.'

It was Susie, entering unannounced. Her face was pale and there were the ravages where tears had been, but there were no tears left now. She was dignified and in control, and she introduced herself and took Marcia's place by Lachlan's side as if it was her right.

'I'll show you the garden,' she told him. 'I'm sure Marcia and Hamish have business to attend to.'

'I should go back online,' Marcia agreed, and Susie gave her a bright and brittle smile.

'Of course.'

'I'll go back to the search,' Hamish said softly, but the look she directed at him had no trace of a smile left in it.

'It's no use,' she told him. 'Taffy's dead. She's been out all night. If the nocturnal owls didn't kill her, the wedge-tail eagles will have by now.' She turned to Lachlan. 'I'm sorry I wasn't here to greet you. Marcia says you'll be thinking about converting the conservatory to a swimming pool before any sale is made. You need to see it. I'll take you.'

'Susie, you don't need to think about that,' Hamish said uneasily, and received a flash of anger for his pains.

'I know I don't need to think about it, Lord Douglas,' she snapped, emphasising his title with a short, harsh syllable. 'My plane leaves tomorrow afternoon and after that this is all your business. This castle is in the hands of the heir. That's you. And you're going to sell it and put the money in the bank.'

'Which is the only sensible place for it,' Marcia interspersed.

'It is,' Susie agreed dully. 'Of course it is. So, shall we see the possible site for your luxury swimming pool, Mr Glendinning?'

'Susie, go look for your puppy,' Hamish said desperately, and she looked like she wanted to slap him.

'My puppy is dead.'

Then why wasn't she crying? Hamish thought. She should be crying. He'd know what to do if she cried.

What was he saying? He wanted a woman to cry?

'We'll show Mr Glendinning the conservatory together,' he said, gently now, but her anger was increasing.

'We'll do nothing together.'

'Susie…'

'Let her go,' Marcia said. 'She's got the time, Hamish. Surely you have better things to be doing.'

What? he thought blankly. What?

'I'll go back to the beach.'

'Give it up,' Marcia said wearily. 'Didn't you hear Susie? The creature's dead.'

The creature.

He was supposed to be marrying this woman.

He thought of Taffy last night, sitting plump on her bottom and howling her displeasure.

The creature.

'We have no proof she's dead,' he said, to the room in general. 'If you'll excuse me, I'll keep looking until we're sure.'

And he walked away and left them to it.

Why hadn't she cried?

All that long day Hamish watched Susie move

like an automaton. She spent a long time with Lachlan, detailing the castle to his satisfaction. She worked in the kitchen, feeding the searchers. She did a bit more searching herself but her back was obviously paining her. She was limping badly and when Kirsty decreed she should stop, she stopped. She went back to packing, the pile of stuff she was discarding growing higher and higher.

'I'll ship Ernst and Eric over to you,' Hamish said at one stage, and if looks could kill, he'd have been dead right then.

'I've changed my mind. They'd never be at home with me in America. They belong at the foot of the stairs and if you want to shift them…well, that's your business and I don't want to know about it.'

'Susie, stay a little longer,' he urged.

'Why?'

'We don't know about Taffy.'

'We do know about Taffy. Cut it out, Hamish. I'm leaving.'

She wouldn't budge.

At dusk Marcia came to find Hamish. She met him on the way upstairs to change. He'd been bashing through thick bushland in an increasingly hopeless search for Taffy, and he was filthy.

'We need to take Lachlan out to dinner,' she said.

'He's spent the day photographing the castle from every angle—not that you'd have noticed. Honestly, Hamish, your behaviour has been less than civil. He's staying at the pub tonight. It'd be better if we could put him up here, but I dare say you won't ask the widow to do that.'

'Do you have to call her the widow?'

'You know who I mean.'

'I won't ask Susie to have another guest on her last night,' Hamish snapped, wondering again how he'd never noticed how insensitive Marcia was. 'It's bad enough that we're here. Jake and Kirsty are bringing dinner. Susie needs her family and no one else.'

'Then you and I should at least take him out to dinner. You're not Susie's family.'

He wasn't. Hamish hesitated. Marcia was right. He should give Lachlan dinner. And…would Susie want him to be around tonight?

But Kirsty came through the front door then, carrying a casserole.

'Hi,' she told them. 'Dinner in thirty minutes?'

'We're going out to dinner,' Marcia said, sounding efficient.

'Oh?' Kirsty raised her eyebrows. 'You, too?' she asked Hamish.

'Um…'

'I shouldn't put pressure on you,' Kirsty told him. 'But it would be better if you were here tonight.'

'Why?' Marcia demanded. 'Why should Hamish stay?'

Kirsty looked a bit taken aback at that, as if she hadn't actually expected an argument.

'To leaven the loaf,' she said at last. 'Susie's miserable. We've searched a two-mile radius and Taffy's nowhere. Taffy was supposed to be the little bit of Dolphin Bay she was taking away with her. Now there's just Susie and Rose.'

Not even Ernst and Eric, Hamish thought, leaning back on a suit of armour. Welcoming the sharp dig of a halberd in the small of his back.

'Susie will be better off without a pup,' Marcia said sharply. 'The fewer encumbrances, the better.'

Kirsty looked at her thoughtfully. Appraisingly. Then glanced sideways at Hamish, leaning wearily on his halberd.

'You're taking the assessor, Lachlan, out to dinner?' she asked Marcia.

'That's right.'

'Then can I ask that you, Marcia, take Lachlan out to dinner, and you, Hamish, stay here and see if you can cheer Susie up. Wear your kilt or something.'

'I suspect there's not a lot that'll cheer Susie up,' Hamish said.

'No,' she admitted. 'But we can try.'

Hamish hesitated.

Marcia looked at her watch. She tapped her foot. She looked at Hamish and saw indecision. Or maybe…decision. There was one thing that could always be said about Marcia: she was good at sussing which way the wind was blowing. She was excellent at not wearing herself out fighting the inevitable.

'I'll go, then,' she said, visibly annoyed. 'Honestly, Hamish, someone has to keep a business head on their shoulders in this whole debacle.'

'They do,' he agreed, but he was watching Kirsty, seeing Kirsty's disapproval, thinking how very like her twin she was. Was Susie vibrating with the same disapproval?

Probably not, he thought. She'd be in her bedroom, sorting the last things she wanted to take from this place. She'd be thinking of Angus, or of Taffy, or of walking away from her vegetable garden and leaving her wonderful conservatory to be ripped apart. There'd be no room in her distraught mind for disapproval of one dumb would-be earl.

'You're not spending more time looking for the dog?' Marcia was demanding, looking at him as if she didn't know who he was any more. Which, come to think of it, was pretty much exactly how he was feeling about himself. 'Everyone's saying it'll be dead.'

'She'll be dead,' Kirsty said softly, and the look she gave Hamish then was slightly doubtful. 'But we'll give the grounds one more sweep after dinner.'

'Miracles don't happen,' Hamish said flatly, and Kirsty gave him another odd look.

'We'll see. We certainly have enough pumpkins around here for a spell or two to happen.' She shook herself, obviously perturbed that she was getting fanciful. 'OK. I have a full casserole dinner ready to be brought in from the car, provided by the ladies of Dolphin Creek. Any crisis round here, sick baby, lost puppy, can't solve yesterday's crossword, you'll be handed a casserole—so we have, at last count, eleven. Marcia, if you and Lachlan aren't joining us, we'd better start now. We have a lot of eating to do.'

It was a very strained meal. They had eleven casseroles. Between them they ate about half of one, and that was with Kirsty and Jake's twins helping. The two little girls were the only bright company during the meal, but even their chatter was pointed.

'Daddy, why does Aunty Susie have to go back to America?'

'That's where her home is.'

'But her home is here.'

'This castle belongs to Lord Hamish now,' Jake told them gently.

'But everyone says Lord Hamish doesn't want it.'

'Lord Hamish doesn't have to want it,' Susie told the girls, with only a hint of a tremor in her voice. 'It's just the way things are. It's his, and I don't belong here any more.'

'But you're our Auntie Susie,' Alice said tremulously, and Penelope agreed.

'We want you to stay. And you haven't got a puppy to take home now. You'll be really, really lonely.'

'I'll have Rose,' Susie said, her voice strained to breaking point. She rose to fetch the coffeepot from the stove and started to pour. 'Coffee, Hamish?'

'Please.'

'None for me,' Kirsty told her, and Susie stilled. She'd been facing the stove. Now she turned, very, very slowly, to face her twin.

'You always have coffee after dinner.'

'I… Not now.' Kirsty seemed all at once uncomfortable and Susie's face grew even more blank.

'I was right,' she said, and her voice was devoid of all expression. 'At the fair. You deflected me with Taffy and I was so preoccupied I let myself be deflected. You're pregnant.'

'Oh, Susie,' Kirsty said, her face twisting in distress.

'That's lovely news,' Susie managed, and stooped

to give her twin a hug. But there was no joy, Hamish thought, watching the tableau in incomprehension. What was going on?

'I so didn't want you to find out.'

'Until when?' Susie turned back to her coffee cups.

'I thought…until you were settled back in America.'

'Won't this make a difference?' Hamish asked, concerned. They both seemed on the edge of tears, but there were no tears. Just rigid control.

'Sure,' Kirsty said coldly. 'Ask Susie to stay because I'm pregnant? How could I do that to her?'

Easy, Hamish thought, remembering his mother and his aunts. He knew exactly how emotional blackmail was done.

'I won't ask for the same reason Susie hasn't asked you not to sell the castle. Not to destroy the greenhouse. I bet she hasn't, has she?'

'No, but—'

'And if I did and you agreed?' Susie said, suddenly fierce. 'How do you think that'd make me feel for the rest of my life? And if Kirsty thought I was staying now just for the baby…she couldn't bear it. That's why she hasn't told me. I don't know where you come from, Hamish Douglas, but we don't do emotional blackmail here.' She swallowed and turned her back on him, facing her sister again. 'You're due when?'

'Not until November. It's early days yet.'

'If I can, I'll come back.'

'Of course you will.'

'To stay?' Hamish said cautiously, and got another glare for his pains.

'To visit. Like normal people do.'

'But you guys are twins,' he said, feeling helpless. 'You should be together.'

'They'll be together for the birth,' Jake said, putting his hand across the table to reach his wife, taking Kirsty's hand in his and holding it firmly and with love. 'If I have to sail across the Atlantic single-handed and haul Susie back here in chains, I promise you'll be together for the birth. I'm covering the expenses and if Susie argues, then she'll see what brothers-in-law are really made of.'

'Oh, Jake,' Susie said, choked.

And Hamish thought, Here at last come the tears. But they didn't. Susie stared at her sister and her brother-in-law for a long moment—and then went back to her coffee-making.

With one mug of hot chocolate for the expectant mother.

CHAPTER TEN

KIRSTY and Jake and assorted kids left soon after. The arrangement was that they were taking Susie to the airport the next day—Jake had organised medical cover for the town from a locum service so both doctors could leave. They took all the kids home with them to give Susie a clear run with her packing.

'We'll be here at eight tomorrow to pick you up,' Kirsty told her twin.

'I'll be ready,' Susie promised.

And Hamish thought once again, Why didn't she cry? She should be crying.

She cried at pumpkins. Why didn't she cry now? Suddenly he thought he wanted her to cry. It'd be OK if she cried, he decided. It was the set, wooden expression on her face that he hated.

He stood in the hall and waited while she waved them off from the front step, and he was waiting for her as she returned.

'What would you like me to do?' he asked softly, and she glanced at him with suspicion.

'Nothing.'

'I'll go down to the beach, then,' he said. 'Just for a last check.'

'Taffy's dead.'

'You don't know that.'

'Yes, I do. I'm not stupid. Ten-week-old puppy in this terrain... I see things how they are, Hamish. Not how I want them to be.'

'You should be able to hope...'

'I gave up on that when I buried Rory,' she said flatly. 'Now, if you don't mind, I have things to do.'

'Can I help you pack?' He should butt out, he thought. He was adding to her distress just by being here. He felt so damned helpless...

'I would appreciate help in Angus's room,' she said, and then looked as if she regretted saying it.

'What needs doing in Angus's room?'

'It's just...' She hesitated. 'I've never cleared it out. I mean, it all belongs to you but I thought...his personal stuff...most of it needs to be thrown away but I don't want Marcia doing it.' The last few words were said in a rush, fiercely, and he thought she'd burst into tears but she didn't. She was pale and almost defiant, tilting her chin as though expecting to meet a fight.

'Marcia's the least sentimental of all of us,' he said mildly and her chin came forward another inch.

'All the more reason why she shouldn't be the one who takes care of it.'

So on a night when she should be doing her own personal packing, when the last vestiges of the search party made vain sweeps of the beach and the hillside looking for Taffy, when Kirsty and Jake cared for the kids so Susie could spend one night alone with her memories, she and Hamish sat on Angus's bedroom floor and sorted...stuff.

Stuff.

Deirdre's stuff and Angus's stuff. The old man hadn't cleared his wife's things, and everything was still there.

The clothes were easy. They'd go to the welfare shops. Hamish could be trusted with that so, with the exception of Angus's kilt and sporran and beret, they were bundled into boxes to be carted away.

But the kilt and beret and sporran... 'I don't know what to do with these,' Susie whispered, holding up a kilt that was far too small for Hamish.

Hamish fingered the fabric, watching the graceful fall of the pleats, thinking of the times Angus must have worn this, the number of fêtes he'd opened in this town, the affection in which he'd been held.

'Is there a local museum?'

'No.'

'A library maybe?'

'Yes...'

'Then why don't we donate it as a display?' he suggested. 'I could donate the cost of a display cabinet. We could put Angus's and Deirdre's photos in it, photos that show them as they were, vibrant and having fun, and set this costume up beside it. Do you think the locals would like it?'

There was a moment's hesitation. Had he said the wrong thing?

Would she cry?

She didn't cry. 'That'd be wonderful,' she said in a small voice. 'Can I leave it with you to see that it's done?'

'Of course.'

She nodded, a brisk, businesslike little nod that had him wishing, wishing she'd falter a little, give him room...

Room to what?

'I'm not marrying Marcia,' he said into the stillness, and her head jerked up from the papers she was sorting.

'You're what?'

He hadn't even known he was going to say it. He hadn't even really thought about it.

Or maybe he had.

He'd approached marriage to Marcia as he approached business propositions, he thought. The marriage would be advantageous to both of them. But these last few days had been like the switching on of a lightbulb in a dimly lit room. Suddenly he could see colour where before he'd only seen grey.

Suddenly he'd not only stopped fearing emotion, he was thinking a bit more emotion wouldn't be such a bad thing.

Like Susie crying so he could hug her better?

'Does Marcia know you're not marrying her?' Susie asked. Her head lowered again, and her voice dulled. She was in a grey world of her own right now, he thought, methodically packing stuff into boxes, lifting Angus's papers, checking them, putting unwanted ones in a pile to be burned. Shifting the detritus of a past life. Absorbed in her own misery.

'I'll tell her tonight.'

'I'd appreciate it if you left it until I was gone. She's going to blame me.'

'Why should she blame you?'

There was a twisted smile at that. 'I'm a corrupting influence,' she said dryly. 'I make you leave your Blackberry at home when we go to the beach.'

'That's a good thing, too,' he said stoutly and then

watched her for a bit more as she went back to sorting papers. 'Susie, do you have to do this? I can do it after you leave.'

'Angus would want me to. I should have done it before this. I just…I couldn't bear to.' She hesitated. 'Will Marcia be upset, do you think?'

He thought about it. Would Marcia be heartbroken? No. But maybe her pride would be hurt. 'I think maybe I should have told her before I told you,' he said ruefully.

'Yeah, she'd hate that. Well, forget you told me. I'll forget I know.'

'I need you to know,' he said softly, and it was true.

Silence. She bent her head over her sheath of documents. A pile of notepaper, pastel blue.

More silence. Where was he going here? He didn't know.

Five minutes ago he'd been engaged to Marcia. He still could be, he thought, confused. What he'd said didn't have to go out of this room. It wasn't irrevocable.

But it was irrevocable, and the more he thought about it the more irrevocable it seemed. Engaged? He wasn't engaged to Marcia. Engaged meant entwined, linked, connected. He surely wasn't entwined, linked, connected to Marcia.

Tonight he'd watched Kirsty and Jake over the

dinner table. He'd seen their eyes meet as they'd shared their distress. And that glance… It had been nothing, but it had meant everything.

He wanted that sort of communication with the woman he married. He didn't want to share a beach-towel with a laptop.

'Go to bed,' he told Susie, softly because he wasn't sure what his head was doing—where his thoughts were taking him. He needed time to think this through.

'These are personal. I need to sort them.'

'I'll pack them up and send them to you.'

'No. You pack the clothes.'

'Susie, you need to pack your own gear. The way you're going you won't get to bed tonight. It's not as if you can sleep on the plane. Rose will be a full-time job.'

'That's not your business,' she snapped.

It wasn't. But, hell, he couldn't bear to see this.

'There's nothing so personal—'

'These are letters,' she cut across his protest, fiercely angry. 'These are personal letters.'

'Then maybe we shouldn't read them at all.'

'No.' Her anger faded a little at that, but the pain seemed to remain. She was kneeling on the floor by Angus's bedside cabinet, papers spread around her. Still in her shorts and T-shirt, with her hair tangled and wisping round her face—the last thing she'd thought of today had been brushing her hair—she looked absurdly young. How could this slip of a girl be a mother? Hamish wondered. How could she be a landscape gardener by herself? Susie against the world?

'Listen to this,' she said softly, and he paused in his folding of sweaters and let himself watch her face again. She was holding herself rigidly under control, he thought, so rigidly that at any minute it seemed she might crack.

'Listen to what?'

'I know…well, maybe I know that we ought to burn these without reading them,' she whispered. 'But Angus knew he was dying, and he left them. So maybe…maybe…'

'What?'

'Maybe he didn't mind us reading them. Maybe he was even proud of them. This is from Deirdre. Way back when she was shopping for the contents of this castle. We're talking forty years back.'

'It's not too personal?'

'You need to know a bit of back-story,' she told him, ignoring his query. 'Angus put a huge amount into this castle, because building it provided an industry for the men of the town in a time of recession. But the locals say he scared himself with how much it cost, and when it came to furnishings he turned into a real scrooge.'

'I can't imagine the Angus I've heard about being tight with his money,' he said, and Susie's face softened in agreement.

'Neither can I. But listen to this. Deirdre's obviously in the city on a buying spree, writing to Angus back home.'

My love, we have children!

Angus, darling, it's one of the great sadnesses of our marriage that we haven't been blessed with babies and we can't adopt. Well, I've found a replacement. No, sweetheart, I haven't picked up a couple of strays, much as I'm always hopeful a couple will come our way. But today I've found Eric and Ernst.

Who are Eric and Ernst? I can hear you say it in increasing trepidation. Irish wolfhounds, maybe? Diggers up of vegetable gardens?

No.

They're warriors. They stand eight feet tall in their gauntleted—is that what you call it?—feet. They're a sort of made-in-Japan imitation suit of armour, real and ready to fight, lifelike right up to the eyes in their visors—white glass eyes with a little black pupil that bobs up and down when you lift the visor up and peer in. I found them in the back of a theatre-prop-cum-junk-shop and they're so neglected. Angus, Ernst is missing a leg! Can you believe that? We'll need to build him a new one. Do you know a leg builder? They're shop soiled and tattered and unloved, and I just looked at them and knew they were destined to stay with us for as long as we live.

Anyway, dearest, kindest Angus, this is to say that we're coming home on Friday and if you were planning on meeting the train in your car can you think again? I talked to the nice man at the railways today and he says he can't guarantee they'll be safe in the goods car so I've bought two extra tickets. Ernst and Eric can sit in the carriage with me. Isn't that the best thing? Can you imagine it? Oh, my dear, I'm so excited. I so want you to meet them. You and me and Eric and Ernst, ready to live happily ever after from this moment forth.

There was a long silence.

It was a ridiculous letter.

Hamish thought of Marcia writing such a letter, and couldn't.

He tried to imagine Susie writing such a letter—and could, very, very easily.

Susie and Deirdre. Twin souls?

There were too many twins. His head was spinning.

'Why couldn't she have children?' he asked at last, trying to sound neutral. 'Surely forty years ago adoption was an option?' He was changing the subject here, and he wasn't quite sure what he was changing it from, but he was starting to feel desperate.

'Deirdre was profoundly deaf,' Susie said softly, rereading the letter with a smile. 'I imagine adoption agencies wouldn't see deafness as a desirable attribute in adoptive couples. From what I know of Deirdre, she might have excluded herself on those grounds.'

That floored him. He sat back on his heels and thought of what he knew of Deirdre.

'I thought she was a nurse during the war.'

'She was.'

'How could she be a nurse if she was deaf?'

'She worked in a rehabilitation hospital. I imagine she would have fought tooth and nail to be useful. Lack of hearing wouldn't have stopped her. From what I've heard of Deirdre, she refused ever to stand still. Half the older generation of this town knows some sort of sign language as everyone wanted to talk to her. They tell me she was irresistible. Angus loved her so much.'

The twin thing slammed back again. Deirdre and Susie, taking on life no matter what life threw at them.

'How could they ever have communicated?'

'Without e-mail?' Susie said dryly. 'It's beyond comprehension, isn't it? But Angus said he woke up one morning in his army hospital; she was standing by his bed and she smiled at him—and he just knew.'

'Love across a crowded room,' he said disparagingly. 'Right.'

'One of the other soldiers had lent him a magazine like *Playboy,*' she continued, ignoring his attempt at sarcasm. 'He'd gone to sleep with Bunny of the Month splayed across his chest. He woke and Deirdre was giggling and he thought, Sod bunnies, this is the one I want.'

Sod bunnies.

Susie was smiling again. When she smiled it was as if the sun came out, Hamish thought, and Angus's words slammed into his consciousness with the force of a high-voltage charge.

This is the one I want.

'I don't suppose…' he said into the stillness, and then paused.

'You don't suppose what?' She was back to sorting, her head down, her curls falling forward, intent on the task at hand.

'I don't suppose you'd like to marry me?'

There was complete and utter silence in the room, and the silence lasted for ever.

What had he said? The words rang round and round in the silence, echoing over and over. He hadn't meant to say them, he thought wildly. They were just suddenly—there.

'Marry,' Susie said at last, and she sounded like she'd been winded. 'You're asking me to marry you.'

'Yes.' He thought about it, wondering what on earth he was saying, but somehow the words still sounded right. His proposal might have been made on the spur of the moment, but that was definitely the gist of what he'd been asking.

'And you're asking me to marry you because?' Susie demanded. She had her breath back now, and was sounding politely bemused. Which was wrong. He didn't want her to sound politely bemused.

'I suspect I'm in love with you,' he managed, and listened to what he'd said and thought, Yep, that sounds OK, too. He sounded confused—but then he was feeling confused. About some things.

Not marriage. He was sure about this.

'You're engaged to Marcia.'

'I'm not marrying Marcia.'

'Marcia thinks you're marrying Marcia.'

'I've made a mistake,' he said. 'Jodie told me I was making a mistake and I didn't see it. It's only now—'

'Who's Jodie? Another fiancée?'

'Jodie's with Nick. He's a woodcarver.' He thought about the way Jodie had said goodbye to him, the way she'd dared him to take this holiday and move on.

Jodie would be proud of him.

'So you moved on to Marcia?'

'Jodie's my secretary.'

'She's still in your life?'

'Susie, can we get back to the issue at hand?'

'Which is that you'd like to marry me.'

'Yes.' This was dumb, he thought. He was sitting on one side of the room in a tangle of sweaters and socks. She was sitting on the far side of Angus's bed, surrounded by papers. He should be down on one knee on her side of the room. At the very least they should just have had a candlelit dinner—not the Country Women's Association Tuna Surprise.

He thought of the finesse of his proposal to Marcia and the dinner that had preceded it and he almost grinned. But not quite. A survival instinct was kicking in here, telling him that chuckling over cliché engagement settings wasn't quite the thing to do right now.

'Why do you think you love me?' She still had the conversational tone. He'd like to move closer but her words...they were like a defence, he thought. A bit brittle. A bit too casual.

'Susie, I don't want you going back to the States by yourself.'

'I'm not going by myself. I'm going with Rosie.'

'You know what I mean.'

'I'm not sure what you're suggesting here.' She still hadn't moved and neither had he. It was like some crazy, stilted conversation about something that concerned neither of them. 'Are you saying you want me to stay here and you'll stay, too—or are you saying you want me to come back with you?'

He hadn't thought that far ahead. He tried to make his mind work, but there was something akin to fog blanketing everything. Making it impossible to apply logic.

He was terrified, he thought suddenly. He was just plain terrified. Stepping off into some abyss…

'Hey, Hamish, I'm not going to accept,' she said gently. 'There's no reason to look like that.'

'Like what?'

'Like I'm a cliff edge,' she said gently. 'I won't do that to you.'

'You're no cliff edge.' But he'd been thinking that. How had she known?

'You don't really want to marry me.'

'I do.' This seemed important. If he kept saying it then it'd start to make sense, he decided. It must make sense.

'What would you do with me?' She almost sounded amused. 'Back in Manhattan?'

'You could work. There's all sorts of landscaping jobs.'

'Window-boxes to be planted out. That sort of thing.'

'We'd get a place further out,' he said, starting to sound as dopy as he felt. 'I can commute—or stay in Manhattan during the week and come home at weekends.'

'In the tiny gaps you have from work.'

'At least you wouldn't be alone.'

She let her breath out in a long exhalation. She looked at him then, really looked at him—and then she pushed herself to her feet.

'Hamish, this is crazy. You haven't thought it out. Forget you said it. It's time I went to bed. I'll get up early and see how much of this I can cope with then.'

She was letting him off the hook, he thought, but he didn't want to be off the hook. Sure, he hadn't thought this through, but the essentials were there. He rose with speed, crossing to stand before her, reaching out to grasp her wrists and hold her at arm's length.

'Susie, it could work,' he said urgently.

'Don't be daft.'

'I'm not daft.'

'If you didn't feel sorry for me,' she said softly, 'would you be even thinking of marriage?'

'No, I—'

'That's what I thought,' she said flatly and hauled her arms back.

'No!' His word exploded across the room, frightening in its intensity. He took her hands in his, urgent. 'Susie, it's not like that.'

'It's not?' She swallowed, seemingly as confused as he was. Struggling to figure things out. 'If I wasn't limping, would you be thinking you could possibly let Marcia down?'

'I can't marry Marcia. Not feeling as I do about you.'

'But you're talking about commuting. In the gaps from work. In the same breath as a proposal. To stop me being lonely.' She took a deep breath and carefully, carefully disengaged her hands. 'Hamish, when I was single I loved having my own space. I had lots of friends and loneliness didn't come into it.'

'But you're lonely now.'

'Because I met Rory,' she said softly. 'When he and I were together there wasn't loneliness. How could there be? Sure, there were nights when we were forced to be apart, but our phone bills were enormous and we'd go to sleep talking to each other. Thinking of each other.'

'As you and I—'

'Shut up and let me finish,' she told him, and her voice was almost kindly. 'Because it's important. Rory died and I learned what loneliness is. It's the awful, awful emptiness when people leave.'

'Susie…'

'It gets filled,' she said, almost conversationally. 'Now I'm alone I've gone back a little to how I was. I depend on me for my company. It's taken two years but I've learned to cope. But, you know, Kirsty comes to dinner, and then she leaves and the loneliness closes over me again. I fell for Angus and it was good, but when he died, it was bleakness all over again. Emptiness. You know, there are lots of single people who don't like people staying overnight because the house seems so empty when they're gone. Loneliness happens again and again and what you're offering… Hamish, every time you walked out the door I'd be alone.'

'I'd have to work,' he said, startled, but she shook her head, as if she was sad about his incomprehension.

'Yes, but when you went to work I wouldn't come with you.'

'What the—?'

'In your heart,' Susie whispered. As he stared at her in confusion, she smiled. 'Hamish, you don't understand and maybe if I hadn't had it with Rory then I wouldn't understand either. But Hamish, I've fallen in love with you.'

She'd fallen in love... He reached for her but she took a step back, holding up her hands to ward him off.

'No.'

'No?'

'No,' she said softly. 'If you think that makes a difference...'

'Of course it makes a difference. I've fallen for you, too, Susie.'

'Have you?' she said. 'You've spent your whole life defending yourself, learning not to let anyone close, and you're not about to stop now. You're going to spend our entire married life waiting for me to manipulate you. If I was fool enough to marry you. Which I'm not.'

'I know you won't manipulate me.'

'No, you don't. You don't know anything about me.'

'I know you're the most courageous person I've ever met.'

'That's pity,' she said flatly. 'Not love. If I died tomorrow, would you cry?'

'I don't cry,' he said before he could stop himself, and she stilled.

There was a long, long pause.

'No, she said at last. 'You don't cry.'

'Susie, I'm not emotional.'

'Well, there you go, then,' she said softly. 'Maybe we're a match after all, because neither am I.'

'Are you kidding?'

'You see, that's the problem,' she whispered. 'What you see is on the outside. You're thinking you might marry the outside. But inside...you don't have a clue. You just don't have a clue. And now, if you'll excuse me, I'm going to bed.' She made to push past him but he stepped across the doorway.

'Susie, please, think about it. It'd be sensible.'

'It'd be committing me to loneliness for the rest of my life,' she whispered. 'Even I think I deserve better than that.'

CHAPTER ELEVEN

WAS she mad?

Susie lay and watched the shadows. This was her last night in this castle.

The man she loved had asked her to marry him.

A courageous woman would take him on and train him, she thought desperately into the stillness. Marry him and ask questions later. Have a tantrum or six when he spent fourteen-hour days at the office seven days a week and treated her as being on the outskirts of his life. Which was what would happen. She was under no illusions as to how Hamish saw marriage.

He'd had some sort of epiphany this week, she thought. He'd seen Marcia out of her business zone and seen how sterile the life they proposed was.

So he'd gone for the easy solution. The noble one. Ditch the businesslike fiancée and pick up a ditzy one with a gammy leg and attached child. Give his life a bit of interest and do good along the way.

Problem solved.

She rose and crossed to the window, staring out at the moonlit sky. An owl swooped across the night sky and she thought of Taffy. Taffy…

She'd had her for what? A whole day? And she'd gone, and Susie felt…

Sick.

'This is it,' she whispered into the dark. She wanted Rose here so she could hug her, so she could tell her baby she was doing the right thing. 'I can't expand my heart any more. The heart expands to fit all comers? Maybe, but how often can it break and stay intact?'

She wanted to cry but the tears wouldn't come. Nothing would come. She should sort a few more things. She should…

Dammit, if it's not packed now I don't want it,' she told the moon fiercely, watching the flight of the owl over the water's edge. 'I've got no more room. I have no more room for anything.'

'Marcia, I can't marry you.'

It was two in the morning. Hamish had been sitting at the kitchen table, waiting for Marcia to come back. Which had taken quite some time. Now she'd burst in the back door, still laughing, and had stopped dead when she'd seen Hamish waiting.

He should have broken it gently, he thought as her laughter stopped. He'd been sitting here for hours, trying to make it right in his head. Nothing made sense any more, but the only absolute that stood out was what he'd just said.

He couldn't marry Marcia. In the end the words had just come.

'What? What have they told you?' Marcia demanded, and he blinked.

'Pardon?'

'Hell, this place! How did they know?'

He blinked again—and then he focussed. She looked rumpled, he thought. There was sand in her hair. A strand of dried seaweed was intertwined with the normally impeccable French knot.

The knot was coming undone. She put a hand up to adjust it, a pin came loose and it tumbled free.

What was going on?

'You've been on the sand dunes?' he ventured cautiously, and she swore and shook her hair looser, causing a shower of sand to fall to the floor.

'God, who'd live in a small town? People have been staring at me since I hit the town boundaries. I might have known.' She glared across the table at him, defiant. 'What do you mean, you can't marry me? You're not getting prudish on me, are you?'

'Prudish?'

'I was bored, OK? There's nothing to do in this god-forsaken place and you were stuck with the widow.'

'So...' He was putting two and two together and making six. But maybe six was right. 'You and—Lachlan?—headed for the sand dunes.'

'Of course Lachlan. Who else do you think? Hell, Hamish, someone had to be nice to him. You hardly made the effort.'

But she had coloured. His efficient, cool fiancée was seriously flustered.

'You were nice to him...as in heading for the sand dunes.'

'It was just a bit of fun! This is the modern world, you know.'

'I think I'm old-fashioned.'

'Well, don't be. Hell, Hamish, we lead separate lives. That's the basis of our whole relationship.'

'What relationship?'

'We fit,' she snapped. 'You know we do. Together we can be a serious team. But not if you're going to get jealous every time I let my hair down.'

'I would have thought...maybe you'd want to let your hair down with me?'

'Oh, come on, Hamish. That's not what our relationship's about. We're a *serious team*. Does it matter if we get our fun elsewhere?'

And it was as easy as this. He was being let off a hook he hadn't known he was on until tonight, and suddenly he didn't even recognise what it was that had snagged him.

She didn't love him. He didn't love her. Where on earth had they been headed?

'I'm in love with Susie,' he told her, and she paused in shaking her hair to stare at him in incredulity.

'You have to be kidding.'

'I don't think I am.'

'What on earth do you have in common?'

'I guess…nothing. Are you in love with Lachlan?'

'Of course I'm not. I don't do love.'

'Including with me?'

'We're a sensible partnership,' she snapped. 'You know that. We've talked about it. You let emotion into your life and it's down the toilet. If you were on with the widow—'

'I'm not on with anyone.'

'But you want to be? With her?' Disbelief was warring with incredulity that he could be so stupid.

There was only one answer to that. 'Yes.'

'She'll never be a businessman's wife.'

'Maybe I'll be a landscape gardener's husband,' he retorted, and she gave a crack of scornful laughter.

'This is ridiculous. You're being ridiculous.'

'Yes.'

She paused. Regrouped. 'Let's talk about this. We don't need to break up. I want that title,' she said abruptly, as if it was suddenly the most important factor in the whole deal.

'I think you can buy titles over the Internet if you pay enough,' he said cautiously. 'I'll see what I can do. It can be a breaking-off-engagement present.'

'You're not serious.'

'I'm serious.'

'I've come all this way for *nothing?*' It was practically a yell. She was no longer flustered. She was out and out furious.

'I'm sorry.'

'Not half as sorry as you're going to be,' she snarled.

'You really think I wouldn't mind a marriage where my wife trots off into the sand dunes with other men?'

'This has nothing to do with anything I might have done with Lachlan,' she flashed back. 'Has it?'

'No,' he admitted. 'It hasn't. But I've decided… Marcia, maybe emotion is important in a marriage. Maybe we could both do with some.'

There was a long pause, strained to breaking point.

'Right,' she said at last. 'You want emotion? Let's see how you deal with emotion, you stupid, two-timing wannabe country hick!'

Sitting in the middle of the table was a vast earthenware casserole containing the congealing leftovers. Marcia removed the lid. She lifted the pot—

and she threw the entire contents at her fiancé's head.

With pot attached.

Tuna surprise!

Susie heard Marcia come in. She heard their soft murmurs in the kitchen. Then the voices were raised. Then came a crash of splintering crockery.

Should she get up and investigate?

Mind your own business, she told herself, and shoved her pillow over her head so she couldn't try to eavesdrop.

She didn't want to know.

She didn't.

Breaking off his engagement had been as easy as that.

Hamish lay in bed and stared at the ceiling and wondered where to take it from here.

His cell phone rang.

It was three in the morning. Was there an emergency back in the office?

'Douglas,' he said crisply into the phone, trying to sound efficient, and there was a sigh down the line that he recognised.

'You're not supposed to be working.'

'Jodie?'

'You remember me?' His ex-secretary sounded pleased. 'Nick said you mightn't answer the phone if you recognised my number. Are you still in Australia?'

'Yes,' he said cautiously. 'Jodie, it's three in the morning.'

'Since when did you need sleep? I've just seen your photograph.'

'My photograph,' he said blankly.

'Oh, Hamish, it's lovely.'

'Aren't you supposed to call me Mr Douglas?' he demanded, and her sigh this time was totally exasperated.

'I'm not your secretary any more. I'm calling as a friend.'

'Why?'

'To tell you I think she looks gorgeous. To say the baby looks really cute and the dog's amazing and I've never seen you look so happy. I opened the magazine and got such a shock that I almost dropped my coffee.'

'What magazine?'

She told him and he gaped into the stillness. 'How...?'

'You're on the beach,' she told him. 'The baby's asleep at your feet. What's the dog's name?'

'Boris,' he said, before he could stop himself. His mind was racing. A photograph on the beach. Albert and Honey... It had to be Albert and Honey's photograph. This was Susie's doing. She'd told them his real name, they'd have done some research, and now the photograph would be splashed across America.

Did he mind?

'Is she nice?' Jodie was asking.

'Um…yes.'

'One of the girls from the office told me Marcia was following you.'

'Marcia's here. Jodie, what business is it of—?'

'You see, the thing is that I'm pregnant,' Jodie said, ignoring his interruption. 'I thought I was last week and now I'm sure. Nick and I are so happy. But I'm so happy that I want everyone else to be. So I'm worrying about you.'

'You don't need to worry about me.'

'I won't if you end up with the lady on the beach.'

'She won't have me,' Hamish said before he could stop himself, and there was a breathless pause.

'You've fallen in love,' Jodie said at last. 'Oh, Hamish…'

'She won't have me.' It was almost a statement of despair. He was in territory here he didn't recognise.

'You haven't asked her to live in your grey penthouse?' Jodie said anxiously. 'She doesn't look the sort who'd live in a penthouse.'

'Hell, Jodie, it's where I live. It's where I work.'

'I've taken a job as part-time secretary in the

church that Nick's restoring,' Jodie said as if she hadn't heard him. 'The pay's lousy. Not a lot of prestige there. I'm happy as a pig in mud.'

'I'm pleased for you. But—'

'Don't stuff it, Hamish.'

'Mr Douglas!' he roared before he could stop himself, and there was a cautious silence—and then a giggle.

'You've got it bad,' she said on a note of discovery. 'Oh, I'm so pleased I phoned. Nick said I was butting in where I wasn't wanted but I so wanted to know, and now I do. I'll ring you back in a few days and find out the next installment. Don't stuff it. And don't shove your penthouse down her throat.'

Where was sleep after that? Nowhere. The castle was almost eerie in its stillness. At five Hamish rose and went out into the bushland behind the garden. He walked the trails in the moonlight, calling over and over again.

'Taffy?'

If he could find her…

He wasn't sure what that might mean. He only knew that Susie was holding herself under rigid control and he needed to break through it. Somehow. If he could find Taffy, he could offer to buy a house on the coast, commuter distance from work. He could see Susie there, but the loneliness thing was an issue. She'd need a dog.

He could buy her a dog but Taffy would be better. Taffy was dead.

But there was a tiny part of him that was refusing to accept the pup's death. It was the logical conclusion and he'd spent his entire life trying to be logical, but he'd just let this tiny chink of inconsistency prevail. Just for now.

'Taffy…'

He didn't find her. Of course he didn't find her. Logic was the way to approach the world. Logic was always right. Emotion…well, it had no place in his life. Did it?

There was a bruise on the side of his head that said emotion was happening whether he encouraged it or not.

Somehow he had to persuade Susie anyway, but by the time he conceded defeat and returned to the castle, he knew he was too late.

The castle was alive with people. Half Dolphin Bay seemed to be there. Kirsty was presiding over the kitchen, issuing orders. A mountain of luggage was piled in the hallway. Susie was behind a mug of coffee, with half a dozen women sitting around her.

She looked up as Hamish entered. Their eyes met—
and he saw a tiny flicker of hope die behind her eyes.

'You didn't find her.'

She knew what he'd been doing. She wasn't being
logical either. She was still hoping.

Someone had to see things as they were. 'No.' He
spread his hands, helpless. 'Susie…'

'Hamish, can you help Jake load gear into the
car?' Kirsty asked, sounding as if she was annoyed
with him, and he met her gaze and knew he was
right. She was seriously displeased. 'It's like a huge
jigsaw puzzle. How we're going to fit everything in,
I don't know.'

'Sure.'

'And what happened to Mrs Jacobsen's casserole?' Kirsty asked.

'I took a dislike to it. Tell Mrs Jacobsen I'll buy
her ten more. Susie, can I talk to you?'

But Susie was no longer looking at him. 'I'm
leaving in half an hour and I have all my friends to
say goodbye to,' she whispered. 'Hamish, we said
everything we needed to say last night. There's
nowhere else to go.'

'Susie, you're way over the limit for cabin baggage.' It was Jake, appearing at the door and looking
exasperated. 'Rose can't need all these toys.'

'One's Hippo, one's Evangeline and one's Ted.

They're all too precious to be entrusted to the cargo hold.'

'You'll have to repack,' Jake said, trying to sound stern. 'Evangeline weighs two kilos. Two kilos for a toy giraffe! It's either Evangeline or the nappies.'

Susie closed her eyes, defeated by choice. Blank.

She should be crying, Hamish thought, feeling desperate. She should be sobbing. But her face was closed and shuttered. Dead.

'Please, Susie…' he started, and her eyes flew open again.

'Leave me be,' she snapped, anger breaking through the misery. 'Hamish Douglas, butt out of what doesn't concern you.'

If there'd been another casserole to hand he could have been hit twice over. And maybe he would have welcomed it.

He butted out.

Marcia was packing as well. He went out to the courtyard and found her loading her gear into the back of Lachlan's BMW.

'As fast as that?' he asked, and she gave him a vicious glare. Lachlan, looking nervous, stayed back.

'You don't want me here. I'll be back to you about financial details.'

'Financial details?'

'This has cost me,' she muttered, throwing a holdall into the trunk with vicious intensity. 'I've wasted three years of my life organising our future and you mess it up with one stupid widow. If you think you'll get out of that without a lawsuit, you have another think coming.'

'You did go to the sand dunes,' he said mildly. He looked across at Lachlan, who decided to comb his hair in the car's rear-view mirror.

'I hate you,' Marcia told him.

'You don't do emotion.'

'I so do!' She rallied then, whirling to face him head on, and her eyes were bright with unshed tears. Tears of fury, frustration and bitterness.

'You see?' she snarled, her voice almost breaking. 'I do "do" emotion. It's just that I don't want to. It stuffs up your life. You can't control people. And I don't want it, any more than I want you.' She flung herself into the passenger seat and slammed the door. Unfortunately the window was open and without the engine on she couldn't close it.

'Get in,' she snapped at Lachlan. 'Let's get moving.'

'Sure,' Lachlan said, and grinned at Hamish. 'That's quite a lady you're losing.'

'Rich, too,' Hamish offered.

'You think I don't already know that?'

I'm sure you do, he thought as he watched the BMW disappear from view.

Two unemotional people?

No. There were emotions there all right. Maybe they were in the wrong place but they were still there.

As were his. He just had to figure out where to put them.

He still hadn't figured it out thirty minutes later as he watched Susie climb into Jake's car. Still with no tears. Still with that dreadful wooden face he was starting to know—and to fear.

'Goodbye, Hamish,' she said, but she didn't kiss him goodbye.

Her body language said it all. He had no choice.

He stood back and let her go.

The castle emptied, just like that. One minute there'd been a crowd waving Susie off, a confusion of packing and tears and hugs and waving handker-chiefs as the car disappeared down the road.

Then nothing. The inhabitants of Dolphin Bay simply turned and left, went back to their village, went back to their lives. Which didn't include him.

Hamish went back into the kitchen, expecting a mess, but the Dolphin Bay ladies had been there *en masse* and everything was ordered. Pristine.

There was a note on the table from Kirsty.

Susie's organised professional cleaners to go through the place tomorrow. Leave a list of what you want kept. They'll dispose of the rest. Mrs Jacobsen says one casserole dish will be fine, thank you, but it had better be a good one.

Great.

He walked back out to the hall where Ernst and Eric were looking morose. Guard duty with nothing to guard.

They'd look dumb back in Manhattan, he thought. Could he write a clause into the hotel sale, saying the new owners had to keep these two?

Ridiculous.

The word hung.

Why had Susie thought his proposal ridiculous? It had been a very good offer, he thought. He'd told her he loved her. He'd look after her, keep her safe, make sure she wanted for nothing.

Ernst and Eric gazed at him morosely.

Ridiculous.

'The whole thing's ridiculous,' he snapped. 'Not me. What does she want me to do?'

Whatever it was, he couldn't do it. He couldn't.

His phone buzzed and he looked at the screen. Jodie. Another lecture.

He flicked it off. Out of communication.

That meant the office couldn't communicate either.

Good. He needed to not communicate.

'You are sure you're doing the right thing?'

'Of course I am.' They were outside the vast metal gates at the airport—gates you could only go through as you passed passport control. The days of waving planes off were long gone. Now the gates slammed on you two or three hours before the plane left and that was that.

Susie and Kirsty were in a huddle. Jake was standing back, holding Rose, giving his wife and her sister space to say goodbye.

'But you're in love with Hamish.'

'He doesn't have a clue what love is. Leave it, Kirsty. It's over.'

'You will come back when our baby's due?'

'I promise.'

'Oh, Susie, I don't see how I can bear it.'

'If I can bear it you can,' Susie said resolutely. She'd expected to be a sobbing mess by now, but the tears were nowhere. She didn't feel like tears. She felt dead.

'I can bear it,' she told her sister. 'You've been the

best sister in the world but we're separate. Twins but separate. You have your life and I have mine.'

Yes, thought Kirsty as she stood and watched the gates slide shut, irrevocably cutting Susie off from return. I have my life. My husband, my kids, my dog, my life. Oh, Susie, I wish you had the same.

What the hell was a man to do?

Hamish paced the castle in indecision. He went back into Angus's room and looked at the papers scattered over the floor. Yes, they needed to be gone through. There were all sorts of important deeds that couldn't be left. They represented a couple days' work.

He'd stay for two more days, and then he'd leave.

He rang the airline and booked his return flight for two days hence. Right. That was the start of organisational mode.

Now sort the papers.

It didn't happen. His head wasn't in the right space. The papers blurred.

He went back out into the garden and saw his half-finished path. He's work on that.

Two spadefuls and he decided his hands were just a wee bit sore to be digging.

He'd go to the beach. He'd swim.

Alone?

He had to do something.

He went to the beach.

The water was cool, clear and welcoming. Before, every time he'd dived under the surface of the waves he'd felt an almost out-of-body experience. It had been as if he'd simply turned off. A switch had been flicked. Here he could forget about everything but the feel of the cool water on his skin, the power of his body, the sun glinting on his face as he surfaced to breathe.

Today it didn't work. He couldn't find a rhythm. He felt breathless, almost claustrophobic, as if this place was somehow threatening.

Susie had almost lost her life here, he remembered. And he hadn't been here to help her.

She wouldn't have let him near even if he had been here.

Hell.

He looked back to shore. A sea-eagle was cruising lazily over the headland. As he watched it stilled, did a long, slow loop, focussing on something below, and glided across the rocks just by him.

There was something there—a dead fish maybe—but Hamish's presence distracted the bird. For a moment he thought the bird would plunge down, and suddenly he splashed out and yelled at it.

The bird focussed on him and started circling again. Slowly.

Still watching whatever it was on the rocks.

It'd be a dead fish, Hamish told himself. Nothing but a dead fish.

He struck out for the rocks, surfacing at every stroke to make sure the bird wasn't coming down. Twelve, fourteen strokes, and he reached the first of the rocks. They were sharp and unwelcoming. He'd cut his feet trying to get across them.

It'd be a dead fish.

But the thought wouldn't go away. He looked skyward and the bird was focussed just in front of him. Two or three yards across the rocks.

He hauled himself out of the water. Ouch. Ouch, ouch, ouch.

A dead fish…

It wasn't a dead fish. It was Taffy, curled into a limp and sodden ball, half in and half out of a rock pool.

He thought she was dead. For a long moment he stared down at the sodden mat of fur, at the tail splayed out in the water, half floating. At the little head, just out of the water.

And then she moved. Just a little, as if she was finding the strength to drag herself out of the water an inch at a time.

The rocks were forgotten. His feet were forgotten.

He was kneeling over her, lifting her out of the water, unable to believe she'd still be alive.

'Taffy,' he whispered, and her eyes opened a little. And unbelievably the disreputable tail gave the tiniest hint of a wag.

'Taf.' He held her close, cradling her in his arms, taking in the enormity of what had happened.

What *had* happened?

He looked up and the eagle was still circling. There was another bird now, swooping past, as if the two birds were disputing about who was to get lunch.

Two birds…

He looked down at Taffy and saw lacerations in her side. Deep slices. Something had picked her up…

And carried her out over the sea? And then maybe got into an argument with another bird, and the prey had been dropped.

If she'd been dropped into the white water around the rocks then maybe the birds had lost her. Maybe she'd have been left struggling in the water, to finally drag herself up here.

Only to expose herself again to the birds of prey who'd dumped her here in the first place.

Hamish was crying. Hell, he was crouched on the rock and blubbing like a baby. Taffy.

'We'll get you warm,' he told the pup. 'We'll get you to a vet.'

But to walk over the rocks in bare feet was impossible. He was two hundred yards from the beach.

He'd have to swim.

He backed into the water, dropped down into the depths and felt Taffy's alarm as she was immersed again. He was on his back, cradling the pup against his chest. He'd get back to the beach using a form of backstroke—backstroke with no arms? But if the pup struggled...

'Trust me, Taf,' she said softly, and it seemed she did. The little body went limp.

'Don't you dare die on me,' Hamish told her. 'I have such plans for us. My God, how can I have been so stupid?'

The doors closed behind her.

It was over. Susie walked past the duty-free shops and the huddles of excited travellers and she didn't see them. Her mind was blank.

'I'm not going to let myself get depressed again,' she told Rosie, hugging her almost fiercely. 'I've been down that road and never again. If I'd let Hamish have his way...no, I've fought too hard for independence to risk it all over again.'

That was the crux of the matter. Maybe she could change him. Maybe she could teach him what it was to really love.

'Oh, but if I failed...' she told Rose. 'I have you to think about now, sweetheart, and I'm just not brave enough to risk everything again.'

The vet was stunned. And beaming.

'Two deep lacerations on the right side but only scratches on the other—the bird couldn't have got a decent grip. But there's nothing vital damaged. We'll run an IV line for twenty-four hours just to be on the safe side but you've got her warmed and dry. I see no reason why she shouldn't live to a ripe old age.'

Hamish stood and stared at the little dog on the table and felt his knees go weak. He'd run up the cliff, wanting help, wanting to shout to the world that he'd found her. The castle had been empty.

He'd opened the oven door, lined the warm interior with towels and laid the pup in there while he'd pulled on some clothes. Then he'd offered her a little warm milk, and had been stunned when Taffy had hauled herself onto shaky legs, shrugged off her towels and scoffed the lot.

Then he'd thought that maybe he'd done the wrong thing in giving her milk—maybe she'd go into shock or something—so he'd bundled her off to the vet. To be given the good news.

'She's as strong as a little horse,' Mandy, the vet,

was saying. 'Susie will be so pleased. I can go about sorting out the quarantine requirements again.'

Taffy would leave, Hamish thought blankly. Of course. Taffy was Susie's dog.

She didn't feel like Susie's dog. She felt like family.

'Can I take her home?' he asked.

'Back to the castle? Can you keep her still so the IV line stays in place?'

'Sure.'

He carried her out into the morning sunshine and shook his head, trying to figure where he was.

Things had shifted. Important things.

What plane was Susie on?

He started doing arithmetic in his head. The new rules for international flights meant you had to be there three hours ahead of departure. Kirsty and Jake's car had been overloaded, and they'd left leeway, expecting delays. If he left now…

Taffy was in a box in his hands, the IV line hooked to a bag slung over his shoulder. He'd have to rig it up carefully in the car to get her back to the castle.

He didn't want to go back to the castle.

He'd have to find someone to care for Taffy.

He didn't want someone else to care for Taffy. At least…not completely.

'You haven't found the puppy?' It was Harriet, Dolphin Bay's postmistress, emerging from the post office and carefully adjusting a sign on the door to read 'Back in Five Minutes'. 'Oh, my lord…'

'I'm not *my* lord,' he said absently. 'I'm Hamish.'

'You're my lord to me,' she said, resolute. 'Ever since I saw you in that kilt.' She peered into the box and her mouth dropped open in shock. 'You've found her,' she whispered. 'Oh, my lord. Where was she?'

'An eagle had her,' he said, but he was moving forward. 'Harriet, see that sign?'

'The sign?' She turned back to where she'd written Back in Five Minutes. 'Yes?'

'Can you make it five hours?'

She looked at him as if he was crazy. 'Of course I can't.'

'Yes, you can,' he said encouragingly. 'I'm your liege lord. You just said it. My wish is your command. Harriet, I command you to change the sign, hop into the front of the car and cuddle Taffy.'

'Why?'

'Your liege lord needs his fair lady.'

'Flight 249 to Los Angeles is delayed by sixty minutes. We wish to apologise for…'

'Fine,' Susie said to Rose, and glowered at the screen. 'Let's go buy some duty-free perfume. You'd like that, wouldn't you, sweetheart?'

'No,' said Rose.

* * *

'What do you mean, she can't come in?'

'Sorry, mate, dogs are forbidden in airport premises.' Hamish had parked the car in the multi-storey car park and they were now at the airport doors. Hamish was carrying Taffy's box and Harriet was carrying the IV line.

'You can't go any further,' the man said, and Harriet sniffed, knowing what was coming.

'Harriet…'

'You're going to ask me to sit in the car with Taffy,' she said darkly. 'Just when it gets interesting.'

'Harriet…'

'Don't mind me.' She sighed, her bosom heaving with virtuous indignation. 'I'm just the peasantry.' Then she grinned. 'Go on with you,' she told him. 'But I'm not staying in the car. I'll just sit on the doorstep here and watch the comings and goings. Taffy and me will like that.'

'You can't stay here,' the security officer told her, and she puffed up like an indignant rooster ready to crow.

'There's a sign saying I can't come in with dog,' she said. 'But there's no sign saying I can't look in with dog. That's just what I'm doing.'

And she sat on the rack holding the luggage

carts in place. She slung the IV bag over her shoulder, she took Taffy's box into her arms and she smiled.

'What are you waiting for?' she demanded. 'Go fetch who you need to fetch.'

Her flight had been delayed. Oh, thank God, there was sixty minutes' grace. But even then it wasn't easy. There was the little matter of the metal doors at passport control.

'You can't come through,' he was told. 'Not unless you're a traveller.'

'I'm a traveller.' He hauled his passport from his wallet and displayed it. 'I'm from the US.'

'You need to be booked on a plane today. You need seat allocation before you can get through.'

They were adamant.

'We can get a message to whoever you want to see,' he was told. 'But if they come out they'll have to go through security again. No one will be happy.'

Maybe she wouldn't come out, he thought. Maybe a message wouldn't work.

He took his wallet over to American Airlines. 'I have a ticket two days from now,' he told them. 'Any chance of swapping it for today?'

'The flight's fully booked,' he was told. The girl

behind the counter eyed him dubiously, and he thought that even if he had been booked there might be trouble. He'd dragged on jeans, a windcheater and trainers but he hadn't shaved that morning and he'd come straight from the beach.

And he knew he looked desperate.

Hell.

The gates stayed shut. She'd be through there, sitting, miserable, maybe crying…

He stared at the screen. There was Susie's flight, leaving in forty-five minutes. Any minute now they'd start boarding.

The flight straight after that was to New Zealand.

Susie's flight was from Gate 10.

The New Zealand flight was from Gate 11.

Act cool, he told himself, trying frantically to be sensible. If you launch yourself at the counter and act desperate, they'll drag you off as a security risk.

So he sped into the washroom, washed his face, bought a comb and a razor from the dispenser and spent precious minutes transforming himself from a beach bum with hair full of sand to someone who might board an international flight with business in mind. Casual but cool.

He stared at himself in the mirror. What was missing?

Ha! Five more precious minutes were spent buying a briefcase and a couple of books to bulk it up.

Then a walk briskly to the Air New Zealand counter, feeling sick with tension and with the effort not to show it. 'Any chance of getting onto the flight this afternoon? I only have hand luggage. I'm booked for a US flight in two days but I've finished what I need to do here and could usefully see some of my people in Auckland.'

His authoritative tone worked. The girl looked him up and down—and smiled. 'Do you have a visa?'

He did. The work he did required travel at a moment's notice and he always had documentation.

'There's only economy available,' she said, and he almost grinned. What value a comb?

'Thank you.'

Which way was New Zealand?

Why would she want to buy perfume?

'Let's have a look at duty-free cigarettes.'

'You don't smoke,' she told herself.

'I might. If I get desperate enough.'

'Are you all right, madam?' an assistant asked, and she blushed.

'Um…yes. Just telling my daughter about the evils of smoking.'

* * *

Hell, why was security taking so long? The line stretched forever.

'Passengers for Air New Zealand, please come through the priority line.'

Thank God for that. But when he was through…

'They're boarding already. If you'd like to board the cart we'll get you straight to the boarding gate.'

Fine. But he was jumping off early.

She wasn't in the departure lounge.

Where was she?

'This is the final boarding call for Flight 723 to Auckland…'

Where was she?

'Pardon me, sir, your flight is ready for boarding. You need to come this way.'

'Not until I find who I'm looking for!'

There was a commotion down near her boarding gate. Shouting. Beefy security men, running.

Then a couple of burly giants escorting someone back toward the entrance area.

Susie glanced up from her rows of Havana cigars…

Hamish.

'Excuse me,' she said faintly, stepping out into their path. 'Where are you taking him?'

'Security,' one of the guards said brusquely. 'Step aside, ma'am.'

She was holding a box of Havana cigars in one hand, Rose in the other. She dropped the cigars.

With huge difficulty she managed to hold on to Rose.

'You can't take him away,' she said faintly. 'He's mine.'

CHAPTER TWELVE

'So you see, you need to come home.'

They weren't going anywhere right now. The chief of airport security had raised his eyebrows, shrugged and shown Hamish, Susie and Rose into his office, closing the door on three trouble-makers.

'Take her baggage off the plane,' he growled to his staff as he left them to it. 'American Airlines is already boarding. She's officially missed the plane and if she objects I'll have them booked for nuisance. Or something.'

But there was no way she'd object. The security head was smiling as he closed the office door behind them—and he just happened to nudge a wastepaper bin full of crumpled paper in Rose's direction. He had kids himself and he knew what was needed here was a bit of distraction so the adults of the party could sort themselves out.

Rose obliged. She immediately started emptying the trash, paper by paper, perusing the security memos of the day with all seriousness, then ripping them into tatters, more thoroughly than any shredder.

Hamish wasn't reading anything. He was holding every part of Susie he could reach.

'But I still don't understand,' she whispered when she could finally find room to speak. She'd just been very thoroughly kissed. She was snuggled against him and he smelt of the sea. He tasted of the sea. Her Hamish. 'Just because you found Taffy…'

'I cried when I found Taffy,' he told her. 'It felt right. And then the thought of sending Taffy to you in America felt wrong.'

'So you're saying…?'

'I want to marry you. I want to marry you more than anything else in the world.' Then he hesitated. 'No. That needs improvement. I already asked you to marry me and you very rightly threw it back in my face. But it's different this time. It's more than just the love thing. Susie, I want us to be a family more than anything else in the world.

'Which means?'

'Reorganising,' he said bluntly. 'Not taking you back to my life. Not being part of your life. Making a new life for all of us where all the pieces fit in a new whole. Where all of us are a part of it.'

'Just because of Taffy,' she whispered, awed.

'Just because of you,' he told her. 'When I found

Taffy, I thought how fantastic it was that I'd found her, and then I thought that I'd found our dog but I'd lost the most important person in the world. Here I was, crying about a pup when my life was gone. And I suddenly realised why you cried—and why you stopped crying. You must love me. You must. Please, Susie…'

'Of course I love you,' she said, and tried to smile. 'How could I not love those knees?'

'A woman with taste.'

She silenced him with a kiss, and the kiss lasted deeply and satisfactorily through the shredding of at least ten more security memos.

It was a kiss where all questions were answered. Where there was no need for words.

It was a kiss where two people found their home.

'The first time I asked you to marry me I was dumb,' Hamish whispered at last, when he could finally find the space to get the words out. She was cradled on his knees and he was holding her as if he'd never let her go. 'But, Susie, I swear this is different.'

'I know it's different,' she said scornfully. 'You think *I'm* dumb?'

'I'd never think you're dumb.'

'You don't mind that I've been married before?'

He answered that with another kiss. 'You don't mind that I almost married Marcia?'

'No, but this is different, too,' she said, trying to be serious. 'Marcia and you…you weren't really engaged. But I did love Rory. I never thought I could love again, but his love, this love…it's just…'

'This is a love for who you are now,' he said, hugging her tight while the world steadied on its axis. 'Are you worried that I'll be jealous of Rory? That I'll make you put away his photographs? Hell, Susie, Rory's part of my family and I need all the family I can get.'

'No, but—'

'Rory is part of who you are,' he told her, refusing to be interrupted. 'He loved you and he cared for you and how can I ever be anything but grateful that he found you out in the wide world and brought you into the Douglas clan?'

'As Angus brought Deirdre,' she whispered. 'And all of us…somehow we're all together. She wriggled on his knee, feeling suddenly like bouncing. The shock was wearing off and what was left was a searing blast of joy so great it almost overwhelmed her. 'Oh, Hamish. Do you think we'll live happily ever after with Ernst and Eric?'

'They expect nothing less.'

'In our castle?'

'Sure, in our castle. With our pumpkins.'

'As in all good fairy-tales.' Her thinking was extending, past the confines of the man she loved to the world outside. 'Where's Taffy now?'

'Out in the trolley racks.'

'Where?'

'With Harriet. Come and see.'

And when they finally found Taffy she wasn't alone. The trolley racks were loaded.

Kirsty and Jake had shown the girls round the airport and had finally emerged to find the postmistress—and dog—in residence. So they'd settled down to wait, too—hoping that Hamish hadn't talked himself onto Susie's flight—and when Susie and Hamish and Rose emerged from the airport, it seemed half Dolphin Bay was waiting for them.

'So you've come back to us,' Jake said, but he wasn't talking to the woman he'd said farewell to a couple of hours ago. He was talking to Hamish, gripping him on the shoulder as a man gripped a friend he hadn't seen for years.

'I guess I have,' Hamish said, thinking of the impossibility of futures broking from Dolphin Bay, and then shrugging and thinking that impossibilities were made to be overcome.

'I guess I have.'

E-mail From: Hamish Douglas
To: Jodie Carmody
Subject: Suggestion

Dear Jodie

Susie and I are delighted to hear you and Nick will be at our wedding next month, here in Dolphin Bay. With your pregnancy and your job as church secretary, we thought you'd be deeply embedded in your choir stalls.

But your letter, saying the stalls are finished and you and Nick are after adventure before the arrival of your little one, set us thinking. Maybe you'd like to share our adventure?

As you egged me on to discover, my life has changed. We have a castle, we have a little girl, we have a dog and we have a pumpkin patch. I have my financial training, Susie has her landscape gardening and we've been looking for ways of putting them together.

I can do some sharebroking from here, easily, with only the occasional trip to New York. But I need a secretary.

Susie can garden here to her heart's content, but she needs people to enjoy her garden and eat her vegetables.

The castle is aging and maintenance is screaming to be done. The conservatory alone needs someone to care for it—some-one who loves wood.

The castle needs people.

So we've decided to open our Castle By The Sea. It will be styled as a Cottage By The Sea, which is a famous holiday camp for children in need. Disadvantaged kids will come to us for the holiday of a lifetime. They'll come in times of family crisis, they'll spend two weeks here, on the beach, learning to garden, learning to farm in the experimental farm Susie's planning. They'll take time out from whatever crisis is in their lives. We've talked to the authorities. We have enthusiasm!

But we need someone with experience with disadvantaged kids. They'll come with their carers, but we'd plan their experience. And— you see, Jodie, I do pay attention—I remember you telling me that Nick is a social worker. That he worked with disadvantaged kids and he loved it. We wondered whether he'd like to dip his toe in the water again.

Jodie, we're not offering Nick a full-time job as a social worker or a woodworker, or you a full-time job as a secretary. Susie and I don't intend to be full-time gardeners or sharebrokers either. But we are offering full-time commitment. What we'd like is for you guys to have a house in the castle grounds—maybe helping build it could be Nick's first job—and for you both to be Share-Castlers. Like share farmers, only different. This castle needs two families. We're inviting you to be our partners.

You don't need to answer at once. Terms need to be negotiated. There's no way I'll let you do this as a temp. What about it, Jodie? Will you share our happy ever after?

Think about it and let us know. With love from:

Hamish and Susie and Rose and Taffy and Ernst and Eric

Text Message from Jodie Carmody to Hamish Douglas

We're on our way. P.S. Who are Ernst and Eric?

MILLS & BOON® PUBLISH EIGHT LARGE PRINT TITLES A MONTH. THESE ARE THE EIGHT TITLES FOR NOVEMBER 2006

THE SECRET BABY REVENGE
Emma Darcy

THE PRINCE'S VIRGIN WIFE
Lucy Monroe

TAKEN FOR HIS PLEASURE
Carol Marinelli

AT THE GREEK TYCOON'S BIDDING
Cathy Williams

THE HEIR'S CHOSEN BRIDE
Marion Lennox

THE MILLIONAIRE'S CINDERELLA WIFE
Lilian Darcy

THEIR UNFINISHED BUSINESS
Jackie Braun

THE TYCOON'S PROPOSAL
Leigh Michaels

MILLS & BOON®

Live the emotion

1006 Rom LP

MILLS & BOON® PUBLISH EIGHT LARGE PRINT TITLES A MONTH. THESE ARE THE EIGHT TITLES FOR DECEMBER 2006

LOVE-SLAVE TO THE SHEIKH
Miranda Lee

HIS ROYAL LOVE-CHILD
Lucy Monroe

THE RANIERI BRIDE
Michelle Reid

THE ITALIAN'S BLACKMAILED MISTRESS
Jacqueline Baird

HAVING THE FRENCHMAN'S BABY
Rebecca Winters

FOUND: HIS FAMILY
Nicola Marsh

SAYING YES TO THE BOSS
Jackie Braun

COMING HOME TO THE COWBOY
Patricia Thayer

MILLS & BOON®

Live the emotion

1106 Rom LP